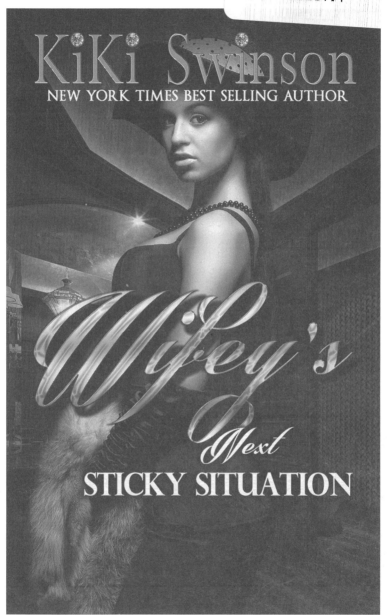

KiKi Swinson

NEW YORK TIMES BEST SELLING AUTHOR

Wifey's
Next
STICKY SITUATION

Publisher's address:

K.S. Publications
P.O. Box 68878
Virginia Beach, VA 23471

Website: www.kikiswinson.net
Email: KS.publications@yahoo.com
Instagram.com/AuthorKikiSwinson
Twitter.com/AuthorKikiSwinson
Facebook.com/KikiSwinson

ISBN-13: 978-0986203
ISBN-10: 0986203

First Edition: October 2018

10 9 8 7 6 5 4 3 2 1

Editors: Letitia Carrington
Interior & Cover Design: Davida Baldwin (OddBalldsgn.com)
Cover Photo: Davida Baldwin

Printed in the United States of America

Don't Miss Out On These Other Titles:

Wifey
I'm Still Wifey
Life After Wifey
Still Wifey Material
Wifey 4-Life
Wife Extraordinaire
Wife Extraordinaire Returns #2
Wife Extraordinaire Reloaded #3
Who's Wife Extraordinaire Now #4
Wifey's Next Hustle
Wifey's Next Deadly Hustle #2
Wifey's Next Come Up #3
Wifey's Next Twisted Fate #4
The Candy Shop 1 - 2
A Sticky Situation
Sleeping with the Enemy (with Wahida Clark)
Heist (with De'nesha Diamond)
Life Styles of the Rich and Shameless (with Noire)
A Gangster and a Gentleman (with De'nesha Diamond)
Playing Dirty #1
Notorious #2
New York's Finest #1
Internationally Known (New York Finest #2)
I'm Forever New York's Finest #3
Cheaper to Keep Her part #1 - #5
His Rebound Bitch #1
The Score part 1
The Mark part 2
Schemes
Most Wanted (with Nikki Turner)
Green Eye Bandit part 1 - 2
Ericka Kane

Wifey's Next Sticky Situation

KS PUBLICATIONS
WWW.KIKISWINSON.NET

ON THE RUN

Nick drove around for five miles before he figured out that he needed to stop by his apartment. "Damn, I need to make a quick stop by my place." He blurted out.

"Do you think that's a good idea?" I asked him. I wasn't having a good feeling about his decision to want to stop.

"I've got no choice. Dylan took the last bit of money I gave him for your ransom so I've gotta stop by my apartment to pick up what money I have left."

"Fuck! Think he had the money on him after he got shot?" I wondered aloud.

"Possibly. But either way, we aren't gonna get it back. There's a lot of cops crawling all over that spot right now. We'd be asking to get arrested if we go back."

"I hope that cop didn't die because if he did, then we're really fucked," I mentioned. I needed for him to be alive or else someone is going to be faced with capital murder charges.

"It ain't gonna matter whether he's alive or not. The cops are gonna pin that shit on us anyway. I mean, who else will they be able to put it on? Dylan and Kendrick are both dead."

"What about those other guys that were there with Kendrick? They were shooting too." I pointed out.

"Trust me, it ain't gonna matter. Those cops are going to make an example out of everyone that was there. So, get ready because the streets are about to get hot." Nick warned me as he raced down the highway.

While Nick barreled his car in the direction of his apartment across town, I couldn't get my mind off Dylan. The images of his dead body began to consume me. The blood from his open wound bled out onto the floor while I cradled his head in my arms. As a result of it, I had a ton of his blood on me. If I allowed anyone to see me like this, they're bound to suspect me of committing a heinous crime.

"Think you'll be able to stop by my apartment so I can get a few of my things? Like clothes?" I wondered aloud.

"Nah, that wouldn't be a smart thing to do. I'm already skeptical of stopping by my place. But I'll tell you what, I'll let you clean yourself up in my bathroom. But you gotta promise not to get any of Dylan's blood on anything in my house. I'm talking about the bathroom sink, tub, floor and whatever else you come in contact with while you're cleaning yourself up."

"I got it," I replied, barely opening my mouth. The thought of losing Dylan and having his blood all over me filled my entire body up with a nauseating feeling. And knowing that I was on the cops' radar added a level of fear to my anxiety. I can't say how I was going to get out of this mess I got myself into, but I will somehow figure it out.

While Nick continued driving, I became more and more afraid of the events that will play out once all the detectives come together and brief one another about what had just happened. My heart rate increased rapidly. And my head started spinning around in circles so I rested it against the headrest of my seat and closed my eyes.

Nick noticed my sudden action and made mention of it. "Does your head hurt?"

I let out a long sigh. "I guess you can say that," I replied, without opening my eyes.

"Just hold on. We are almost at my apartment."

"Your apartment is not what I'm worried about." I continued to say, but this time I lifted my head and

3

opened my eyes. I turned my full attention towards Nick.

"Talk to me." He insisted.

"I'm just thinking about all of this shit we've got ourselves in. I didn't ask for any of this. I just wanted to live a normal life. But no, I had to involve myself in shady business deals that have caused me to be on the run from the fucking cops."

"Look, I know shit is fucked up right now. But I'm gonna find a way to get us both out of this situation, so stop worrying."

"You're making it seem like it's going to be easy," I commented.

"Because it is. Just sit back and trust me." He concluded and then he turned his attention back towards the highway in front of us.

WE NEED A WAY OUT

When we arrived inside the parking garage of Nick's apartment building, we didn't waste any time climbing out of his vehicle. He rushed towards the door of the garage that led to the floor of his apartment. I followed on his heels. "Cover up the front of your shirt." He instructed me right after we entered the building. As instructed, I covered the front part of my shirt and my arms with Nick's jacket. I couldn't cover every inch of the bloodstains, but I made it work. Luckily for me, none of his neighbors were out and about, so we made it into his apartment undetected.

"You know where the bathroom is, so hurry and get cleaned up. I want to be out of here in the next five minutes." He said.

"Okay," I replied and walked away.

After I went into the bathroom, I stood in front of the sink and mirror for a moment just to look at myself. I instantly saw the hurt in my eyes as I stared at

Dylan's blood-soaked in my shirt. I couldn't help it and started crying. I tried to muffle my cry but it became impossible to do. My heart was so heavy with the pain I was carrying. So how am I going to deal with this? How am I going to move forward? And will I ever be able to cope with his death? Because if you look at it, if I hadn't gotten kidnapped, then he would still be alive at this very moment. Not only that, Nick and I wouldn't be packing up our things so we could hurry up and get out of town. Damn! We're truly fucked.

"Kira, I know you're upset. And I know you're hurting but you're gonna have to suck it up so we can get out of here." Nick yelled from the other side of the bathroom door.

I wasn't happy at all about him telling me that I couldn't cry over my man. Was he insane? Or was he being inconsiderate? Either way, he rubbed me the wrong way and my blood began to boil. Instead of being combative, I used the back of my hands to wipe the tears from my eyes. And after I dried my face, I removed the shirt and jacket I wore when I entered Nick's apartment.

It didn't take me long to wipe the blood from my arms and hands and when I was done, I cleaned the area around the sink to make sure that I didn't leave a drop of Dylan's blood nowhere near it.

I grabbed one of Nick's décor bath towels from the towel holder and wrapped it around me. "Nick, I need a shirt," I told him immediately after I walked out of the bathroom.

"I've got one for you here in my bedroom." I heard him say. I followed his voice and headed towards this bedroom. "Put on that sweatshirt." He continued as he pointed towards a Miami Dolphins sweatshirt lying on his bed.

"Thanks," I said as I grabbed the sweatshirt up from the bed. To show some respect for Dylan, I turned around with my back facing Nick so I wouldn't reveal an inch of my breast to him.

The moment after I slipped on the sweatshirt, Nick walked by me and said, "Come on, it's time to go." The urgency in his tone sent a shock wave of emotions inside of me. I was shaken with fear.

"What do you want me to do with my clothes?" I asked him as I followed him.

"Grab a trash bag from the kitchen cabinet."

"Which cabinet?"

"The one that's right over top of the refrigerator." He said as he pointed into his kitchen while stuffing his Gucci Travel bag with clothes he owned.

"We're taking this bag with us, right?" I said while I grabbed a trash bag from the box it came in.

"Most definitely." He insisted as he continued to stuff his travel bag with clothes and shoes.

Immediately after I stuck my bloody clothes in the trash bag, I walked back into the living room where Nick was and stood alongside him quietly.

"Ready?" He asked me after he zipped up his bag.

"Yes," I replied.

"Well, let's go." He said and then he walked towards the front door. I followed suit with the trash bag in hand.

Within a matter of two minutes, Nick and I were out of his apartment and back into his truck. I couldn't believe that we were out of there so quickly. Inside of his truck, he said, "Put on your seatbelt because if the cops get a chance to get behind us, I'm not gonna let them take me down. A'ight!?"

"All right," I said without given his words a second thought. I mean, who wants to go to jail? Not me. And especially behind murder charges. I can't see that happening. I've sacrificed too much to spend the rest of my life behind bars, so I won't be taking door number one.

Nick eased his way out of the parking garage like he entered it, undetected. But as he drove away from his apartment building, three police patrol cars raced towards his building from the opposite direction. This spooked the hell out of me. My heart sunk into the pit of my stomach instantly. "Oh my God! Did you see that?" I asked him while I looked through the back window of his SUV.

He nodded his head. "Damn right, I did."

"God just looked out for us big time."

"Yes, he did. And I thank him for it." He started off, "If we would've stayed at my place another minute longer, we'd be in handcuffs right now." He continued.

"I don't wanna think about them putting me in handcuffs."

"You may not wanna think about it, but when you block it out of your mind, that's when you set yourself up to get caught."

"Why can't we just be optimistic?"

"We can be optimistic. But I'm also a realist and a cat from the streets so I handle things differently."

"And what does that mean?"

"It means that any time you're on the run from the cops, you gotta be at least ten steps ahead of them. I knew it was a matter of time before they would come to my house. I also know that they're probably at your crib right now."

I let out a long sigh after I turned back around in my seat. "How the hell did I get into all this bullshit?!"

"Fucking with Kendrick's grimy ass!"

"Ugh! Why did I feed into his conniving antics? I knew he was a treacherous dude but I didn't think he'd turn on me like he did."

"What made you think that he wouldn't turn on you? That dude shot and killed his own baby mama when she was pregnant with his kid."

"Are you fucking serious? And how come I never heard about that until now?"

"Because no one in the streets talks about it. People fear that nigga!"

"When did this happen?"

"About six years ago."

"Did he get arrested?"

"Nope. I told you nobody talked about it. He had spies in the streets lurking and waiting for someone to open their mouths about it. People were afraid to talk to their own family that they grew up with. That's how crazy it was back when he first murdered her."

"No way. I don't believe that. No man has that much power." I refused to believe.

"You may not believe that Kendrick didn't have that much power, but that story I told you did happen."

"Why didn't you and Dylan tell me this before?"

"Because you didn't tell us that you made a deal with the devil until it was too late." He explained.

"I guess you're right." I agreed. Whether I wanted to agree with Nick or not, I went against Dylan and my better judgment for Kendrick. All I cared about in those moments was the money I made from him by way of commission. It felt good getting $25,000 to $30,000 checks on a monthly basis. If Kendrick didn't stop by the dealership I worked at, then he'd send one of his homeboys and their homeboys would send one of their homeboys. It was a domino effect. Everything was good. But look at me now. Where are the $25,000 checks now? And where is Dylan? I don't have shit now!

While I mulled over all the mistakes I made, I watched Nick as he turned one corner after the next, trying to prevent any of the cops in the area from getting close to us. Driving down one-way streets and back alleys was Nick's way of evading them.

"Are you jumping on Highway 2?" I asked him, even though I already knew the answer. In hindsight, I only opened up a dialogue with him because the silence in his truck was killing me.

"Yeah," he said as we came upon a traffic light. He slowed down and stopped. While we were sitting at the stop light, I watched Nick as he looked through his rearview mirror and occasionally look through the side mirror on the driver side door. But that didn't prepare him for what happened next. "Oh my God Nick, there's a cop car right next to us," I warned him while I watched the car through the right angle of my peripheral vision.

"How many in the car?"

"Just one."

"What is he doing?" He asked while trying to play it cool. I noticed how hard he tried to remain calm while looking at the traffic light in front of us.

"He's looking straight ahead like you are."

"Did you see him look at my truck?"

"No. But I see him on his radio."

"Oh shit! He's probably calling in my license plate."

"Whatcha' gon' do?"

"I'm gonna blow this light in a minute." He said as he kept his eyes on the light.

"Wait, he's moving his car. I think he's trying to see who's in the truck with me." I panicked while my heart felt like it was beating against my ribcage.

"Kira, keep it together. I'm gonna handle whatever comes my way, okay?" He said, trying to assure me.

I took a deep breath and then I exhaled. "Okay, I'm gonna stay calm," I promised him. But as soon as I uttered the word calm, the traffic light turned green and then the cop sounded off his siren. I almost jumped out of my seat. "Fuck that!" Nick blurted out and he sped off through the green light.

As Nick barreled through the intersection I turned around in my chair and I watched in disbelief as the cop car made a sudden right turn at that corner. I turned back around in my seat and faced Nick. "What the fuck just happened?" I managed to say while trying to collect my thoughts.

"He must've gotten a call for something else." Nick offered his explanation as he eased his foot off the accelerator.

"That was a close call," I said while turning my attention towards the cars and buildings we passed by.

"Yeah, it was." He replied as he cruised up the ramp that led to Highway 2.

WHERE ARE WE HEADED TO NOW?

After coming down from what seemed like a panic attack, I was ready to relax a little as he Nick drove further away from his place. "Look, I need you to take me to my car. It's like eight miles from where we are right now." I asked, hoping that my sudden request would force him to react on impulse.

"No, you know I told you...." he began to say but I cut him off in mid-sentence.

"My car isn't at my house. It's parked across the street from my father's bank. That is Kendrick and his boys kidnapped me from.

"So, you wanna take it with us?"

"No. I've got a few things inside my car that I wanna take with me."

Nick let out a loud sigh. "Which bank is it?"

"The one on 14th Street."

"A'ight, but you're gonna have to make it quick." He instructed.

"I will. Don't worry!" I assured him.

I can't quite explain how a nervous wreck I was while Nick drove me to the location of my car, but I will say that I wasn't having a good feeling about it. I was having flashbacks about the incidents that led up to Kendrick and his boys snatching me up and throwing me into a van and drove me away. I was completely caught off guard. I almost even shitted on myself.

At one point while I was in their custody, I thought that they were going to murder me. But thank God, Nick and Dylan came to my rescue. If they hadn't, then there's no question that I would be dead right now.

"Is this the bank you're talking about?" He asked as he slowed down his truck.

"Yes, that's it. And my car is right there," I pointed in the opposite direction of the bank.

"Yo,' is that the fucking police parked beside your car?" Nick said like he was spooked.

Instantly panic-stricken, I zoomed in on the area around my car. "Oh shit! Yeah, that's them. Keep going. Keep going."

15

"What the fuck you think they're doing?" Nick asked me as he continued to drive by my car.

"The way they're parked, makes me think that they're waiting to see if I'll show up to pick up my car."

"How do you think they found your car?"

"They had to have found the bank paperwork inside Kendrick's van."

"What do you mean?"

"I had just come out of the bank after handling my dad's business affairs, so I had money and copies of documents in my purse. When I got to my car, Kendrick and his people grabbed me and threw me in the back of their van. One of the guys wrestled me down to the floor and out the corner of my eye, I saw Kendrick dumping all the contents of my purse out on the floor. And as soon as he saw that I had money, he picked it up and stuffed it in his pants pockets. The rest of my things and my father's paperwork from the bank was left on the floor. So, my guess is, the cops searched their van, found my father's paperwork from that bank, made the connection that I was there, drove over here and noticed that my car was parked in the area." I explained.

"You know we can't stick around here much longer?"

"Yeah, I know."

16

"Good, because I'm getting on the highway right now." He told me.

"Where are we going?" I wondered aloud.

"I'm going up north to my cousin's place. I figured we could lay low there for a few days until I can come up with a better plan."

"Where up north are you talking about?" I asked him. I needed clarity.

"New Orleans."

"New Orleans is north-west."

"North, north-west. It's all the same." He commented.

"Think it's safe to go there?" I wanted to know.

"It's safer than staying in Miami."

"What's your cousin's name?"

"Raymond."

"How old is this Raymond?"

"Thirty-eight."

"He's not into the street life is he?"

"Nah. He's a good guy."

"What's your definition of a good guy?"

"An honest guy working hard to make his money legitimately."

"So, he's one of those guys?"

"Yep."

"You don't work a legitimate job, but you're still a good guy."

17

"Yeah, but he's one of those guys find volunteering at a retirement center for elderly people. Not only that, he's married and he's got a baby on the way."

"How long has he been married?"

"Ten years."

"And you think this family man's wife is going to allow his cousin to bring another woman into their home?"

"Don't worry about Hailey. She's cool. She won't mind." He tried to assure me.

"Yeah, okay," I commented nonchalantly. But I wasn't buying it. Women are very territorial so I can't wait to see how this arrangement works out.

Nick didn't say anything else about his cousin and his cousin's wife, so we both fell silent. I couldn't tell you what was going on in his mind but I can tell you how heavy my heart was. I couldn't believe that I had just lost my man. I also couldn't believe that I was on the fucking run. This was not how I wanted my life to be. My only wish was that I could turn back the hands of time. None of the shit I did to end up in this situation would've happened. I wouldn't have given up any information about my father's friend, the judge. From the day I opened my mouth, everything collapsed into a domino-like-effect. After my father's judge friend was murdered, his wife was murdered second, my old colleague Nancy was the third person to be murdered and then I had to lay my father down to prevent him from implicating me while helping that fucking detective solve the murders that plagued us. Shit, I didn't want any of this mess to happen, but it did so now I've gotta pick up the pieces and try to move forward in my life. I wished my man was still alive to help me move forward, but since he isn't, I've gotta do what I gotta do. Hopefully, I don't get killed in the process. I can only imagine what the news media is going to say after the cops give them their side of the story. *Two suspects have escaped after having a shootout with local police officers. One officer was shot in the process and now he's in the Miami Dade Hospital. It's not clear if he's going to live but we will keep you updated as we receive more information.*

I can see it now; our faces are going to be plastered all over the fucking TV. I just hope that that media clip doesn't make its way to New Orleans. Because if it does, then Nick and I are both screwed.

Nick and I pretty much remained quiet until we crossed the Florida and Georgia state line. "Welcome to Georgia." He said.

"I know that we're not out of the woods yet. But for some reason, it feels like we are." I spoke up.

"That's crazy because I was just thinking the same thing." He agreed as he turned towards me. "Hand me your cellphone." He instructed me.

"Why? Whatcha' gonna do with it?"

"Just hand it to me." He insisted.

I grabbed my cell phone from my pants pocket and passed it to him. Without saying another word, he took my cell phone along with his and threw them both out of the car window. "Whatcha' do that for?" I questioned him after I stared out the back window of the car. I saw both of our cellphones broken in about five to six pieces, lying there in the middle of the highway. I even saw an SUV rollover parts of the phones.

"You do know that the Feds could track our whereabouts with our phones, right?"

"Yeah, but...."

"No buts. If you wanna stay out of jail and off the radar, then you're gonna have to trust me and follow my lead. Okay?"

"Okay," I said and then I turned my head back around to face the traffic in front of us.

Immediately after I put my focus back on the cars driving in front of us, I thought about my man's dead body lying on the floor of that house. My heart instantly filled up with sorrow and that's when the floodgate of my eyes lids filled up with tears. I tried to cry quietly, but I couldn't. I saw Nick through my peripheral vision as he turned his attention back towards me after he heard me sulking. "Awww.... Kira, please don't do that. I can't take seeing you cry." he started off saying while driving, but simultaneously looking for a napkin in his glove compartment and the sun visor over his head. He managed to pull one from his visor. And after he handed that one napkin to me, he started massaging my back with his right hand while using his left one to steer the steering wheel.

"Nick, it feels like my whole world is falling apart. I've lost everything I've loved. And it was all over me running my big fucking month." I spat, wiping away the tears that had saturated my eyes and the cheek area of my face.

"You still have me." He replied, sounding so sincere. The fact that he let me know that he had my back meant a lot, especially after everything that happened back in Miami. "Listen, I know it's gonna be hard, but you're gonna get through this. I'm gonna make sure you get through it." He continued, keeping his eyes on the road before us.

I hate the fact that I was in this fucked up situation. My whole life has collapsed around me. How am I going to pull my life back together? I can't go and turn myself into the cops. And I can't go home and live my life like nothing happened. All I can do now is stay close to Nick and hope that he works this thing out and everything will be alright again.

GOTTA' CHANGE MY APPEARANCE

After driving for 12 hours and over 670 miles, we made it to New Orleans unscabbed. "The ride was long but we're here," Nick uttered from his lips.

I let out a long sigh. "I thought we'd never get here." I chimed in.

"I felt like that a few times too." Nick agreed with me.

"So, how much longer will it take to get to your cousin's house?" I wanted to know.

"We're about ten minutes away." He replied.

"It's 3'oclock in the morning, think they'll open their front door?"

"Of course."

It felt good to hear Nick's answer. I was tired and I wanted to climb into a nice, warm bed. While Nick drove the additional miles that would put us at the address of his family, I couldn't help but think about the cops hiding in wait, hoping I would come back to the bank to retrieve my car. That whole scene scared me to death. Thank God Nick spotted them before they spotted us. What a wake-up call that was.

I also couldn't stop thinking about my father's possessions and how his things could potently be taken from me once they find out that I was on the run. I mean, could they do that? Was it legal? I hope not because it would devastate me if the county police department were able to put seize all my father's belongings being that I was his sole heir.

I also thought about the money I had just gotten from the bank right before I was kidnapped. It sickens me to know that I lost that money too. How stupid could I have been? I should've held onto the money before I exited my car. Ugh! I swear, I've got to make better decisions going forward unless I want to go to jail. And trust me, I don't want that to happen.

When Nick drove into a middle-class neighborhood, I shifted my focus to the quiet, dark roads we were traveling down. "Do they believe in street lights around here?" I commented. I wasn't spooked, but I was close to it.

I noticed the row houses in this neighborhood had taken a colorful and eclectic mind of their own. I wouldn't want to live here because of how closely the houses were built next to each other, but if given the chance, I'd come back and visit.

Parking on the street was the only place Nick could park on this little ass street. By the time he parked his car, I could've run to a local inconvenient store, bought a bunch of groceries and brought them back. The parking was indeed atrocious.

"Hey fam, I'm outside." I heard Nick say after he put a cell phone up to his ear.

"Wait, I thought you threw your cell phone out the window after we crossed the Georgia and Florida state line," I questioned him.

"Yeah, I did. This is a burner cell phone. I got four of 'em."

"Think I can get one? Remember, you threw my cell phone away when you threw yours."

"Don't worry, I got two more. So, as soon as we get in the house and whine down, I'll get one of 'em working for you."

"Thank you," I said and then I followed him towards the front door of the house we were going to hide out in until Nick figures out what we're going to do next.

By the time Nick and I walked onto the porch of this yellow and blue painted house, the door was slightly ajar. And after we walked across the threshold of the front door, we were greeted by a medium build guy standing in a dim lit foyer. I couldn't quite make out his facial features, or the length of his hair, but I was able to see that he had a really nice physic. Nick walked up to him and gave him one of those manly handshakes and the half hug thing that guys do when they greet one another. "Man, I really appreciate you for doing this for me." Nick thanked him and then he stepped aside and introduced me. "This is Kira. My homeboy's girl."

"Hi," I said and shook his hand. I couldn't quite make out his face, but after I shook his hand, and felt the softness, I knew he was a man that had never done a day of hard work.

After standing there for a few seconds, he instructed Nick and me to follow him to the back of his house. When we entered a room, he turned on the light and that's when I got my first look at him. I got to be honest, he was a very handsome guy. He had a strong resemblance to Lebron James. He didn't have the height like Lebron James, but his facial features were undeniably there. He smiled the moment he got a chance to see me in the light. "Are you sure that's your homeboy's girlfriend? She looks like someone I'd hook up with." He commented flirtatiously.

Nick gave his cousin the evil eye. "Come on now dawg, have some respect. Her man just got murdered like ten hours ago." Nick told him.

"My bad. I was just trying to put a smile on her face." Raymond replied.

"Just show us where we can put our bags." Nick continued as he searched every inch of the bedroom with his eyes.

"Put 'em in the closet to your left." He told Nick.

"A'ight, cool." Nick continued and then he took my handbag from me.

While I watched Nick shuffle things around in the closet, I watched Raymond looking at me from head to toe a few times through my peripheral vision. I shrug it off, especially with all the shit I'm dealing with right now. I say, let him look, just as long as he doesn't touch.

Nick and Raymond said a few more words to each other and then Raymond left Nick and me in the bedroom. By this time, I had taken a seat at the foot of the king size bed. "If you feel uncomfortable, I can go in the living room and lie down on the couch." He suggested.

"If you don't mind, I'd rather you be in here with me. I know this is your family's house, but with everything that happened, I don't want to be by myself."

"A'ight, I'll sleep in here with you, but you're gonna have to let me get that comforter and one of those pillows so I can make me a nice pilot on the floor."

"I can't let you sleep on the floor. You take the left side of the bed and I'll take this side." I pointed out.

"I'm cool with that." He said confidently and then he started taking off his sneakers and disrobing. "Don't get nervous, I'm only taking off my pants." He continued.

"I'm good," I assured him while I kept my back towards him. A few seconds later, he climbed onto the bed but he laid down on the opposite end of the bed. He tugged on the sheet and blanket a little bit, so I stood up for a few seconds so he could get as much coverage as he wanted. When he stopped shifting himself around in the bed, I said, "Want me to turn the bedroom light off?"

"Yeah, that would be great." He told me. So, I walked over to the light switch on the wall near the bedroom door and flicked it off. The darkness consumed the entire bedroom, which was my cue to lay down and try to go to sleep myself.

I didn't use the blanket nor the sheet after I climbed onto the bed. I did lie down on top of the comforter. I did this out of respect for Dylan, not to mention that I also didn't want to get too comfortable. I knew from experience that the only way the police can get next to you is if you get caught sleeping. I refuse to let that happen. But if I decide to close my eyes, it won't be both of them. A wise man should always sleep with one eye open.

ON SOME SHADY SHIT

I knew this bitch wasn't gonna like the idea of me being in her house. I knew that the second Nick told me that his cousin had a wife. So, after I slid out of the bed and used the bathroom, I headed towards the front area of the house where I heard Nick talking to his cousin and his cousin's wife. The moment I peered around the corner and saw that everyone was in the kitchen, I walked towards them and that's when all eyes turned towards me. "Good morning everyone," I said first giving them a half smile.

Nick and his cousin greeted me back immediately, but his cousin's wife stared at me for about five seconds before she said hi. I mean, damn! Why was she staring at me from head to toe? I wanted so badly to ask her that question but I knew that if I had, she and her husband would be ushering me and Nick out of their home quicker than I could blink my eyes. So, instead of giving her a piece of my mind, I smiled and pretended like I hadn't noticed her stank ass look. "You must be Hailey?" I said as friendly as I could.

"Yes, I am." She said like she was the Queen of this castle while I was a commoner.

"It's so nice to meet you. And I wanna thank you for allowing me to be in your home." I said to her in a humble manner.

"You're welcome." She said and for a moment she changed the tone of her mannerism. But as soon as Nick's cousin Raymond commented that any friend of Nick's was a friend of his, Hailey turned her attention to him and rolled her eyes as hard as she could. "You sound a little too excited over there, buddy." She didn't waste any time saying.

"Ahhhh, come on honey. She's family now." Raymond said in a jokingly way. It was plain to see that he had put himself in the hot seat. Thankfully Nick chimed in and went to his rescue.

"He's just happy to see me," Nick said.

"That ain't what I see." She replied.

"He's harmless." Nick continued.

"He better be." Hailey threatened. I could tell that she was nothing to play with. She was a very jealous woman and jealous women aren't to be fucked with. Been there. Done that.

"Mind if I could get a glass of water?" I changed the subject.

"Sure, I'll get it." Raymond offered and then he stood up from the chair.

"No, I'll get it." She said and stood up to her feet, giving Raymond the evil eye.

"No, don't get up. You're pregnant. Let Nick, do it." I insisted.

"Yeah Hailey, let me get it." Nick volunteered as he stood up. After Nick grabbed a cold bottle of water from the refrigerator, he handed it to me and suggested that we go to the living room area of his cousin's house.

Nick didn't think I knew why he suddenly wanted me to follow him into another area of the house, but I wasn't born yesterday. Seconds after Nick and I sat down on the sofa, Hailey mumbled something underneath her breath and then she stormed out of the kitchen. Nick walked out of the kitchen and followed her.

"I hope I didn't start anything," I whispered to him, with intentions to keep Raymond and his wife from hearing what I was saying.

"Nah... you alright. Whatever they got going on doesn't have anything to do with you." He replied. But I wasn't buying into his lie.

While Nick assured me that that little dialog Raymond and I had wasn't anything to worry about, the sound of Hailey ripping Raymond to shreds, contradicted everything Nick had just said. Hailey was chewing Raymond out about his overzealous behavior when I joined them in the kitchen. "Just accept the fact that you were acting thirsty towards her." She scolded him.

"I was only trying to be nice. She just lost her fiancé." He tried to explain.

"So, what are you, her fucking therapist?" Hailey snapped.

"Shhhh…. Stop talking so loud. She can probably hear you." Raymond tried to calm Hailey down.

"I'm not shushing… shit! This is my house." I heard her protest.

"Ugh! You're such a fucking bitch sometimes." He said sarcastically and then I heard him storm away from her.

Nick heard Raymond storm off too. He looked at me and shook his head with an expression of utter disbelief. "I'm so sorry about all of this." He whispered once again.

"No need to apologize to me. I'm a woman. I know what it feels like to sit back and witness your man be flirty with another woman."

"Nah, I don't think he was trying to flirt with you. Raymond is a good dude and he really loves his wife."

"I'm not disputing how much he loves he loves her. All I'm saying is that the worse time to show another woman attention is when you're in the presence of your significant other and especially if she's pregnant. That's a big no-no!"

"Well, since you put it like that, I can see where you're coming from."

"Good. Now, have you had a chance to think about what we're going to do? I would hate for us to put all of our eggs into this basket and stuff start falling apart." I said, pointing in the direction of where Raymond and Hailey were.

"Believe me, I've been wracking my brain about what our next move will be. I don't know when I've not thought about it." He assured me.

"Have you thought about how long you planned for us to be here?" I asked him.

"The way things are going with Hailey and Raymond right now, we may not be here very long at all."

"Well, why don't you go in there and tell her that I don't want her man? I mean, goodness gracious she's flipping out for nothing."

"He'll handle it."

"I hope so," I said and then I took a sip from my bottle of water.

Pressuring Nick to come up with an airtight plan to stay off the radar is extremely crucial at this point. America's Most Wanted is shown on every cable channel so traveling around in the public wouldn't be a wise idea either. In all fairness, Nick and I were walking on borrowed time. It would be nothing for someone to recognize us and make that phone call to the feds. We'd be locked up in seconds if that happened. So that's why it is extremely important for all of us to get along. Because if she wakes up tomorrow morning and tells us that we have to leave, then that's what we'll have to do.

"Let me ask you something," I leaned in closer to him and whispered.

"What's up?"

"What would you do if she came in here right now and tell us to get out of her house?" I continued to whisper.

"I know Hailey. She wouldn't do that." Nick replied adamantly.

"But what if she did it?" I wouldn't let up. I was forcing him to come up with a plan B because whether he wanted to believe it or not, I knew that he and I were here on borrowed time.

He hesitated for a few seconds and then he said, "If she does, then we'll go to a hotel until I can come up with something else."

"Okay," I said. I wasn't too happy about his answer but at least he gave me one.

Nick and I heard Hailey as she continued to breathe down Raymond's neck. But then, when we listened closely, we realized that she wasn't talking about me anymore, she was talking about a different woman. A woman he worked with at his job.

It was somewhat of a relief to hear the conversation about me switched to another woman. But the fact that they were still arguing back and forth began to give me a headache. I sincerely hope that this is an isolated incident because I won't be able to take this arguing shit if it becomes a constant thing. "I thought you said that they were happily married?"

"I don't remember saying, happily. But, I did say that Raymond was a good dude."

I cracked a smile and said, "I could've sworn you said happily."

"Look, all I know is that they've been married for 10 years and that they're happy with their baby on the way. All that other stuff that's going on back there, I had no knowledge of. Now enough about them and tell me how are you feeling, otherwise?" He changed the subject.

"When I woke up this morning, it felt kind of weird waking up in someone else's house. So, I closed my eyes, hoping that I was dreaming. But when I opened my eyes back up, that's when I knew that the state I was in and the feelings I had were real." I replied in a low and calm tone while my eyes filled up with tears.

Nick leaned over towards me and embraced me with both arms. And as soon as I felt the warmth of his embrace, my tear ducts opened like the floodgates. Tears ran down my cheeks like water running from a faucet. "It's okay. Let it out." He encouraged me.

I tried desperately not to cry too loud. Didn't want to alert Nick's cousin and his wife that I was on the verge of having a nervous breakdown. "Nick, what are we going to do?" I asked him in a muffled cry.

"Stop worrying about that. I told you that I was working on something." He answered me.

"But that's not good enough. I need to know something right now." I began to plead with them. "Do you know my heart aches from all the pain and suffering I've been having because of my father and Dylan's death? It's now becoming unbearable to do."

"I know it is. I feel fucked up too. Dylan was like a brother to me. He and I did everything together. There was not a time where he was in a bad situation and I wasn't there to help him out. When I got up this morning, I thought about him. I even came in the living room, sat down on the sofa and wondered what he and I would've been doing right now if he was still alive today. Kira, you know he was my road dog. I trusted him with my life and he felt the same way about me too. I just wish the cops hadn't shown up because he probably would've been alive right now."

While Nick was pouring his heart out to me, Raymond's wife walked into the room where he and I was. "What do you mean, you wished the cops hadn't shown up? Did you have a run-in with the police?" She asked surprisingly and stood there awaiting an answer from either myself or Nick.

My heart dropped into the pit of my stomach after I realized that Hailey heard Nick and I's conversation. I immediately shut down, giving Nick no other option but to answer her question. He gave Hailey an awkward expression and said, "It wasn't nothing really."

"What do you mean, it was nothing? You just said that her man would probably be alive right now if the police had not shown up. So, what about that statement means nothing?" She asked him as she took a couple of steps closer towards us. By this time, she was standing in the middle of the floor with her arms folded.

"Look, Hailey, I really don't want to get into that right now. The less you know the better you are." Nick assured her.

Hailey was not satisfied with Nick's explanation so she yelled for Raymond to join us in the living room. "Raymond, I'm gonna need you to get your ass in this living room right now." She roared.

"What do you want?" He yelled from their bedroom.

"You will find out as soon as you get in here. And I mean get in here now." She yelled back.

Raymond came into the living room a minute and a half later. Hailey jumped down his throat the minute she was an eye contact with him. He stood a few inches away from Hailey while Nick and I sat on the couch like sitting ducks.

"What is going on with these two?" She said while gritting her teeth.

"What do you mean what's going on?" Raymond stood there nonchalantly after he looked at Nick and me.

"I just heard them talking about some kind of run-in they had with the police. And then I heard Nick say that if it hadn't happened, her fiancé would still be alive. So, tell me what's going on?" She reiterated all while looking at Raymond.

"Raymond, I'm sorry dude. You know I ain't trying to create beef between you and your wife, especially since she's pregnant." Nick explained.

"It's all good fam."

"No, it is not, all good. I wanna know what's going on. And somebody is going to tell me right now." Hailey roared. Everyone in the room knew that she was not going to move an inch until they gave her an explanation.

I wasn't going to open my mouth at all. I figured if the truth was going to be told then one of the men needed to do it. But the way things were looking, Nick looked like he wasn't going to say anything either. This put Raymond on the spot. "Look," he finally said, "they got in a little bit of trouble so they wanted to crash out here for a little while so they could figure things out."

"Having a run in with the cops is called a little trouble? Are you out of your fucking mind? I heard Nick tell her that if the cops hadn't shown up that her man would probably be alive. So, tell me the fucking truth before I go ham up in here." She threatened.

"Hailey, calm down. You know you're affecting the baby." Raymond pleaded. Hailey stood there next to Raymond with her hands on both hips while she gritted her teeth. Raymond must've known what that meant because he started singing like a bird. "Look, baby, Nick, and her man got into some beef with the cops when they pulled them over. The cops started acting like assholes and things went downhill from there."

I sat there and watched how Raymond conjured up that story about Nick and Dylan having a Black Lives Matter moment. His story was so convincing, I started believing him until I reminded myself that that incident didn't happen that way because I was there.

Hailey stood there and gave all of us a hard stare. I could tell that she was a little skeptical about Raymond's explanation, but in a weird kind of way, she willed herself to believe him. "Why didn't y'all tell me that before?" She questioned Raymond and Nick both.

"I thought he already did," Nick spoke first.

"Well, he didn't," Hailey replied and then she rolled her eyes at Raymond.

"My bad!" He said, with the most dumbfounded expression that he could muster up.

"Keep something else from me again and see what happens." She warned him and then she punched Raymond in the arm really hard.

"Owww… he whined as he grabbed his right arm with his left hand and cradled it.

"Stop whining like a bitch! Because the next time you keep me in the dark about something involving this house or the company we have in here, I'm gonna go slam off on you. And it ain't gonna be pretty." She threatened and then she left the room and headed back in the direction she came from.

I looked at Raymond and Nick both with an expression of relief after Hailey walked away from us. As a matter of fact, all three of us had facial expressions of relief when she left the room. "You sure know how to tell a great lie," I commented. But I said it, low enough so Hailey couldn't hear me. She has ears of a pit bull. You can't say anything for the fear of her hearing it.

"Yeah, that shit was genius," Nick commented after he cracked a smile.

"Don't talk too loud." Raymond chimed in. "Let's go outside on the front porch." He insisted.

The thought of going outside freaked me out. I wasn't willing to risk somebody recognizing me because Raymond wanted to go outside to prevent Hailey from eavesdropping on our conversation again. So, I opted to stay inside. "I'm good. I'm gonna stay in here." I said and looked directly at Nick, giving him the "You better not leave out of this house" expression. Thankfully, he caught my drift and declined to go outside himself. "Yeah, I think I'm gonna stay inside too." He said.

"A'ight, well cool. We can chill out in here and see what's on TV." He suggested. He was grasping for straws trying to figure out how to brighten the mood in here, especially after Hailey had rained on all of our parades.

After Raymond joined us on the sectional, he picked up the remote control and started sifting through the television channels until he ran cross the Shark Tank television show.

"I like this show." Nick blurted out.

"I like this shit too." Raymond agreed.

I didn't utter a word. I was too consumed with how I was going to live from day to day in this new city. I've heard a lot of good things about New Orleans, so my only hope was that Nick and I will be safe until we can figure out our next move.

REMINISCING

Nick and Raymond and I sat on the sectional and watched Shark Tank and as soon as commercials started rotating they'd start talking about how much fun they had growing up in their grandmother's house. "Remember when I snuck that pretty Indian chick named Bianca in grandma's house while she was at the mall with Aunt Teen?" Nick started off by saying, with a huge grin on his face.

"Yeah, I remember that shit." Raymond agreed, becoming amused.

"But do you remember after I talked her into going upstairs to my bedroom, grandma and Aunt Teen came right back to the house and caught our asses?" Nick continued.

"I remember it like it was yesterday, 'cause Aunt Teen cursed me out for watching your back." Raymond pointed out as he chuckled.

"Sounds like you were a player when you were growing up," I commented.

Nick gave me a modest smile. "Nah, that was Raymond." Nick denied.

"That's bullshit!" Raymond chuckled. "All the chicks in our neighborhood loved Nicholas. He used to get a ton of *I love you* notes on a daily basis when we were in junior high and high school. And what was so crazy about it was that the girls he didn't like, he'd push them off on me."

"Oh really? You were carrying it like that?" I teased Nick. But in the back of my mind, I wasn't surprised that Nick was a ladies' man. He just had that look. That swag. And now that he's a man, he's gotten more handsome and more refined.

"Don't believe this guy." Nick encouraged me.

I smiled.

"Kira, you know I'm telling you the truth." Raymond chuckled.

"I believe you, Raymond," I said.

"So, you're gonna believe him over me?" Nick asked me, trying his best to sound convincing.

"Yes, I do. So, it's okay for you to be humble. That's a great characteristic for any man to have." I added. But before Nick could say another word, Hailey reappeared in the living room. Everyone turned their attention towards her. She stood in the middle of the floor, fully dressed with her purse on her shoulder and said, "I'm going to the store Kira. Wanna ride with me?"

I hesitated for a moment, trying to figure out the best way to tell her hell no. I mean, didn't she just give Raymond hell because he was trying to be hospitable to me? Whether she knows it or not, she has made me feel uncomfortable being here. So again, what could I possibly say that won't offend her?

"I would love to go but I'm not feeling so good right now."

"What's wrong?" She wanted to know.

"Yeah, what's wrong?" Raymond chimed in.

I couldn't believe that she was talking to me like she was genuinely concerned. She just went slam off on me and Nick. Was this bitch a modern-day Doctor Jekyll and Mr. Hyde or what?

"I feel a little nausea." I lied to her while I rubbed my hand over my stomach.

"I've got something in the medicine cabinet that'll help you. Raymond, go to the bathroom and get Kira that nausea medicine from the cabinet over the sink." Hailey instructed him.

Nick looked at me in a puzzling manner but he didn't utter another word. Raymond looked at me as he stood up on his feet. "Why didn't you tell me that your stomach was giving you problems?" He questioned me in a sincere manner.

"Because my nausea has been coming and going. It's gotta be something that I ate on the way here." I lied. I couldn't let Hailey in on one of the reasons I declined her offer to leave the house with her.

"Is there anything I could pick up for you guys?" Hailey wanted to know as she walked towards the front door.

"Nah, I'm good," Nick said.

"What about you?" She looked at me and asked.

"I'm good. But thank you." I told her.

"Well, if you two change your mind then have Raymond call me." She insisted.

"We will," Nick assured her. After Hailey yelled towards the back of the house, letting Raymond know that she was leaving, she opened the front door and left. What a relief it felt to see that woman leave. Every time she's around me, I get nervous. It was something about her that made me feel uneasy. I don't know if it was because I was in her home? Or that I intimidated her with my looks? I figured that whatever it was, it would surely come out sooner than later. In all fairness, I would love for everyone to be able to get along because, in my head, I left all that drama back in Miami. So, taking on more stress isn't an option for me. I literary don't have any more room left in my

47

heart to harbor a whole new set of problems. I plan to get out of this emotional rut I was in and move forward with as much peace as I can conjure up.

"Are you really sick?" Nick whispered.

"No. I just said that so she would leave me alone and go by herself."

Nick was just about to open his mouth and say something when Raymond walked back into the living room. "I looked in the bathroom cabinet and I couldn't find the medicine she was talking about." He said while he stood in the middle of the floor empty handed.

I smiled. "It's okay. I'm good. My stomach isn't aching. I just told Hailey that, so I could get out of going to the store with her." I told him.

Raymond chuckled. "Wow! That was a quick comeback. You really threw her off. You fooled me too. See, what happens when you hang out with this guy too long?" Raymond continued while he pointed his finger towards Nick.

"Don't put me in it," Nick said. He wanted Raymond to know that he had nothing to do with the lie I told.

"Hey cousin, I got weed in the back if you want some?" Raymond changed the subject, still standing in the middle of the floor.

Nick's eyes lit up like a Christmas tree. "You know I'm down," Nick replied.

Raymond turned towards me. "What about you?"

"No, I'm good. I'm not into the weed thing." I told him.

"Well, that means there's more for us," Raymond said jokingly and then he had Nick to follow him to the back porch of this house.

I sat there on the couch and continued watching television. Correction, the television was watching me. I couldn't get my mind off of Dylan. I couldn't get his face out of my head. I couldn't get the thought that we could've helped him get out of that house if we had done things differently.

Then I started thinking back on the times we spent together, the nights we made love, times when he'd surprise me with expensive gifts. He'd kiss me all over until I told him to stop; which were memories that I would always hold close to my heart. I also thought about the times when he and I would get into arguments. Feuds that I would normally win. Thanks to him, he made sure that we never went to bed mad with another. He and I had a solid bond that was unbreakable. The love we shared was so strong that we vowed to never let anyone or anything cripple it.

Without warning tears started falling from my eyes, running down the cheeks of my face. It felt like the floodgates had opened. I tried to wipe away my tears before anyone caught me crying, but my hands weren't moving fast enough. At this point, I stopped caring if someone saw me. I'd been holding in my feelings about the loss of Dylan for far too long. "God, why did you let those cops kill him?" I started talking quietly while I lifted my head up towards the ceiling.

"God, you know Dylan didn't deserve to die. He was a good man." I continued to say quietly, trying to prevent Raymond and Nick from hearing me. I wanted to talk with God on my terms, so allowing Raymond and Nick to eavesdrop wasn't an option. I figured that if I could talk to God in my quiet place, then I could get clarity from God as to how I needed to navigate through everything that was going on. I truly needed guidance, and I knew that God would be the one to give it to me.

Father God, would you please forgive me for my sins? Allow me to humble myself before you, God! I also ask if you'd give me wisdom and understanding as I pray to you right now. You know my heart is troubled. And you know all the pain that I've just suffered because of it. You also know Lord God that I wanna find the right way out of this situation. Because if I don't, I'm gonna walk down a very long and dark road. I know I have not been the best servant for you Lord God, but you know my heart. And you know, that I am sorry for everything that I've done that was not your will for my life. So, as I come to you Lord God and you begin to speak to me, please give me a clear head so that I could I hear your every word. I need your direction in my life. It feels like I'm going in circles right now oh Lord, and only you can bring me out. You know what's going on, and you know the outcome. So, Father God, point me in the right direction and if I try to veer off your path, cripple any and everything that would have me do opposite of your will. I trust you, Lord! I trust you with my life. I want to reign in heaven with you Lord God. You are the author and the finisher of my life. I thank you for loving me in spite of the nonsense in my life. And I thank you for shielding me from all hurt, harm, and danger. I seal all these things in the name of Jesus Christ! Amen!

I don't know how but after I prayed to God, I cried myself to sleep. I found out that I slept for a little over an hour when Hailey came back from the store with her best friend in tow. I kept my eyes closed and pretended to be asleep when they walked into the house. While doing so, I was able to eavesdrop in on their conversation. I listened intently to every word they said. "That's her?" I heard a woman say. Her voice was new and unrecognizable.

"Yeah, that's her," Hailey replied while she shuffled around with what seemed to sound like rattled paper bags.

"She's pretty." The woman said.

"She looks okay." Hailey disagreed.

"So, she came with your husband's cousin?"

"Yep," Hailey said. By this time, they had entered into the kitchen. Hearing Hailey open and close cabinets and the refrigerators was a dead giveaway.

"You better watch out because if her body looks anything like her face, you're gonna be in trouble." I heard the best friend warn her.

"Trouble how? She doesn't look better than me." Hailey stated.

"All I'm gonna say is, make sure she stays fully clothed while she's walking around your house. You can't have her strutting around with skimpy ass clothes, enticing your husband while you ain't around."

"Look she just lost her boyfriend back in Miami because of some Black Lives Matters shit, so trying to entice Raymond is the last thing on her list."

"Wait, hold up. When did that happen?"

"I thought I told you."

"No, you didn't tell me shit." I heard the woman say in a low whisper.

"There's really nothing to say, but that her boyfriend was killed by some cops back in Miami, so Nick felt the need to get her away from there for a little while. You know, take her somewhere so she could pull herself back together and regroup." Hailey explained to her friend.

As far as I could see, this naïve chick had no idea what the hell she was talking about. But I'll let her believe that she knows the whole story concerning me, Nick and Dylan. If you wanna know my personal opinion, I prefer the Black Lives Matters story versus what really happened. I figured the less these people know about me, the better off Nick and I will be.

A few minutes after Hailey and her friend settled into the kitchen, Raymond and Nick both made their way back into the house and joined them. When they passed me on the way into the kitchen, I felt Nick lay his eyes on me. He didn't look at me long, though. The woman accompanied Hailey must've caught his eyes because he spoke to her the moment I heard his feet hit the tile on the kitchen floor. "You leave out of here to go to the store and when you come back, you bring more than just groceries," Raymond commented in a jokingly manner.

"And hello to you too." I heard the woman say sarcastically. And then I heard her chuckled.

"Hello, Janet." Raymond acknowledged her like he dreaded it.

"Whatever Ray, just tell me who this handsome guy is that's standing in front of me," Janet said directly. She wasn't holding back any punches.

"This is my cousin Nick. Nick, this is my wife's best friend Janet." Raymond made the introduction.

"It's nice to meet you." I heard Nick say.

"Nice to meet you too." I heard her reply. "Oh my God! Your hands are so soft." She continued. And that's when I knew that they made hand contact. One part of me suddenly became jealous but then it dawned on me that I shouldn't be feeling this way. Nick wasn't my man so why should I concern myself with whose hands he shakes? I think that not having Dylan around was consuming me. I mean, Nick was the only person I had in my life after the murders of my father, Dylan, mother and sister. So, I guessed that maybe I'm feeling this way because I don't want another woman coming into Nick's life, for the fear of him putting me on the back burner. And right now, that can't happen.

"Thank you. But so are yours." She complimented him.

"Has anyone ever told you how beautiful you were?" He asked her in a flirtatious manner.

She chuckled. "Come on now, that line was so lame. I know you can come better than that." She teased him.

"Wait, so you're telling me that that line wasn't good enough?" I heard Nick laugh.

"No, it wasn't."

"Dag, you're really hard on a brother."

"That's because I'm intrigued." She told him. And when those words sunk into my head, I instantly wanted to jump up from the couch, grab a steak knife the from kitchen drawer and chop this chick up in a million pieces. I mean, she was serving him heavy with the attention and flirtatious behavior and I wasn't at all happy about it. I'm not trying to cock-block or anything, but she was overreaching this thing. She was acting like she wanted to fuck him right on the spot. All I know is that she needs to sit her silly ass in a corner and call it a day. There's absolutely no way I was going to let that tramp get anywhere near Nick. He's off limits, besides the fact that I may have feelings for him, I can't have her in his space clouding his mind. It would throw him off track. I need him to stay focused about why he and I are here and what our next step will be.

Without thinking about it, I made stretching noises like I was waking up. I knew it would alert everyone that I was getting up. Like clockwork, everyone got quiet. So, I opened my eyes slowly. And once I had opened them completely open, I saw everyone staring in my direction. "Hey, sleepy head!" Nick smiled and began walking towards me.

The moment Nick started walking in my direction, Hailey's friend expression turned from a smile to a grit. She wasn't feeling me taking Nick's attention away from her. Well, I tell you what, she better get used to it because he and I have a connection that no one will ever break. "Did you get enough rest?" He asked me after he sat down on the edge of the sofa next to me. I moved over an inch to give him more space to sit next to me.

"I can't believe I fell asleep," I said. "How long was I asleep?" I continued, trying to brew up a conversation with him. And while I did this, I noticed Hailey gritting on me too. They weren't happy about me taking Nick's attention away from them.

"Maybe an hour or so," Nick replied.

"How is your stomach doing?" Hailey yelled from the kitchen. She was still putting away the groceries she'd brought back from the store.

"I'm feeling a lot better. Thank you for asking." I lied.

"Let me introduce you to my best friend." She said, pointing towards her friend. "This is my best friend Cali. Her real name is Calina. But we all call her Cali."

I looked at Cali and got an eye full. She was a very pretty woman. She put me in the mind of a young Jennifer Lopez. There she was standing next to the island in the middle of the kitchen, showing off her video vixen body. Her whole body was manufactured of course. I'm talking about her titties, to her waist, her hips, and her ass. I could see it clear as day that she had to have spent at least $25,000 to $30,000 in plastic surgery costs. And now that I look at her face, she may have had a nose job too. "Hi Cali, my name is Kira."

"Hi, Kira, nice to meet you." She greeted me. She waved her hand at me in an effort so I could see her Rolex watch and Cartier bracelets. She was wearing the new Printed Red Gucci boots that came up to the knees, with a white Gucci t-shirt and a pair of printed Red Gucci shorts. She looked like a runway model. There was no denying that this chick only messed around with guys with a lot of money.

"Nice to meet you as well," I greeted her back. In return, she gave me a fake ass smile. But I didn't feed into her shenanigans. I see bitches like her all the time. The best thing for me to do was to be fake just like her stupid ass.

"I told Cali that you and Nick were going to be staying with us for a couple of weeks, so maybe you could hang out with us sometimes," Hailey suggested.

57

"Sure, I would love that." I lied once again. I wasn't in the least bit interested in hanging out with them. Especially with Cali and her fake ass smile. She acted too thirsty for me. I can't hang around women that want to be the center of attention.

"Thanks, Hailey, that's really nice of you," Nick interjected.

I pinched Nick in his side, suggesting that he needed to shut up. I wasn't going anywhere outside of this house unless I was with Nick. No one else.

TWO NOSEY ASS WOMEN

I sat up on the couch with Nick next to me while Hailey talked all of us to death about plans she's intending to make so we all could hang out together. Get more acquainted. She has no fucking idea that none of what she's saying is going to happen. Regardless if Nick and I were on the run from the cops, we still wouldn't be interested in double dating or hanging out on the town with her and her fake ass best friend. It doesn't matter how good she makes it sound, it isn't going to happen.

"Wanna head back to the back porch?" Raymond asked Nick while Hailey was still running her mouth about stuff I wasn't interested in talking about.

"Yeah, let's do it," Nick replied. And as soon as he agreed to go with Raymond, I pinched his ass in the side again. He knew immediately that I didn't want him leaving my side. So, he looks at me and says, "Want to hang out in the back with us?"

Before I could answer, Hailey, blurted out, "Oh no, you and Raymond can go hang out in the back and Cali and I will keep her company and do girl stuff."

I pinched Nick in his side once more, hoping he'd come back with a helluva rebuttal so I wouldn't have to stay in here with these two phony ass bitches. But it didn't work. Raymond and Hailey both put the pressure on Nick. "Yeah, that's a good idea. Come on Nick." Raymond chimed in.

"Yeah, take Nick's butt outside and Cali and I will entertain Kira in here." Hailey insisted.

I swear, I wanted to tell Hailey to shut the fuck up and mind her own damn business. But I knew that if I had done that, she'd be ushering me and Nick out of her house. Instead, I kept myself calm and kept my mouth closed, all the while hoping Nick would step in for me and convince them otherwise. But guess what? He caved in and let them have their way. And boy was I furious.

"I'll tell you what?" He started off saying, giving me the side eye, "I'm gonna leave her here with you two ladies for a little while and then I'm gonna come back and get her. The air outside feels great and she needs to be outside so she can enjoy it." He finished.

I'm sure he thought that he handled the situation, but he didn't do shit. He dropped the ball entirely. So, the moment I get the chance to tell him about it, believe me, I will.

Immediately after Nick threw me underneath the bus, he stood up and marched his ass to the back porch with Raymond. Boy, was I steaming on the inside. My blood was boiling.

"Come on in the kitchen with us," Hailey instructed me.

As badly as I wanted to tell her no, I got up from the couch and made my way into the kitchen. Cali couldn't keep her eyes off me. She watched me from the time I got up from the sofa, until the time I entered the kitchen and took a seat on one of the bar stools. I started to ask her why was she staring at me? But then I decided against it. This wasn't the place nor the time to get into a cussing match with a woman I just met. It wouldn't go over well with Hailey. She'd probably curse my ass out if I jump down her best friend's throat.

"Kira, want something to drink? I've got sweet tea, orange juice, bottled water, and lemonade." Hailey asked me after she put a gallon of milk into the refrigerator.

"Lemonade would be fine," I told her.

"Got it. One glass of cold lemonade coming up." Hailey replied cheerfully as she pulled a container of lemonade out of the refrigerator. After she grabbed a glass from the cabinet near the stove, she poured me a glass and then she handed it to me. I took a nice size gulp of it and enjoyed it as I swallowed every drop of it. I sat the glass down on the island after I drank another gulp of it.

Immediately after I sat the glass down, I noticed Cali staring at me once again. This made me feel uncomfortable. And I knew that if I called her out on it, things may go in a direction I don't want it to go, so I left well enough alone. "How long have you two ladies been friends?" I mustered up to say, trying to avoid any confrontation with either of these ladies.

"Almost five years," Hailey answered me before Cali had a chance to.

"Cool. How did you two meet?" I said. But at the same time, not giving a damn how long they've been friends. The objective was to stop this dumb bitch from staring at me. She was making me feel really weird.

"We used to work together at a club called Republic Nola. Well, I still work there and she doesn't."

"So, you two are strippers?"

Offended by my question, Hailey spoke up first. "Do we look like strippers?" She asked sarcastically.

"No, I'm sorry. You don't. It's just that anytime you hear a woman say that they work at a nightclub, you normally think that they work as a stripper. Trust me, it's not shade!" I explained. But in all reality, I was being shady. I stopped liking Hailey after she snapped on Nick and I before she left here to go to the store. So, this dig was especially for her.

"Oh no honey, we don't strip. We're bartenders. And we make a bunch of money doing it."

"The closest thing I've done to stripping was doing bottle service. You know, walking around in badass catsuits, carrying expensive bottles of champagne with lighter flares sticking out of the top of the bottles."

"How much do you get paid to do that?" I was curious.

"You mean walk around with the bottles?" Cali asked me.

"Yeah,"

"It depends. On a slow night like Sunday's and Thursdays, I used to get like $200. And on Friday's and Saturdays, I'll to get anywhere from $500 to $1,000. Sometimes more. But now that business has been slow, I'll get anywhere from $100 a night to $300."

"That's still good money. But aren't you afraid to leave work late at night with that type of money?" I inquired.

"Honey, believe me, I can take care of myself." She replied as she patted the side of her Chanel handbag.

"What's in there?" I asked her. My curiosity was killing me.

Smiled and said, "My chrome protector."

"So, you toting steel, huh?"

"Got to. New Orleans is a nice place to live, but we've got our share of crooks too. So, I go nowhere without my Smith & Wesson .380,"

"I hope you got it on safety."

"Of course, I do. I'm a pro with it."

"Have you ever used it?" I pressed the issue.

"No. But I will if I have to." She wanted me to know.

"Have you ever pulled it out on your ex?"

She chuckled. "No."

"She should've. Then that asshole probably would not have cheated on her." Hailey interjected.

"Everybody cheats Hailey," Cali replied.

"Not all men. Raymond wouldn't dare cheat on me."

"I've gotta agree with Hailey on this one because I didn't have that problem with Dylan either."

64

"Oh my, was that his name?" Hailey blurted out.

Caught off guard, by the way, I had slipped up and told these girls Dylan's real name, made me want to kick my own self in the ass. I mean, how did I let my guard down and tell them that? Ugh! I've gotta put my game face back on before I spill all my beans. "Yes, that was his name." I finally answered, but at the same time regretting that I let felt comfortable enough to divulge that information to them. "But can we please talk about something else?" I asked them.

"Sure," Hailey said.

"Yes, absolutely." Cali agreed and then she changed the subject and said, "I heard that most of the men in Miami are rich. Is that true?"

"We've got some."

"Are they drug dealers. Rappers or what?" Cali continued.

"We have a lot of rich entertainers there. The rest of them are drug kingpins and athletes."

"Well, if you know one of those rich guys then hook me up because I am always on the prowl for another rich guy to take care of me."

"I will do just that." I lied to her. Does she really think I'll set her up with a rich guy? She better wake up and smell the coffee. Dudes aren't taking care of women anymore like they used to. What she might want to do is hop on a pole and start shaking her ass.

In my opinion, that's the only she's going to continue wearing Rolexes and Cartier bracelets. "Did a rich guy snag you those Cartier bracelets and Rolex?" I joked. This was my way of digging into her pocketbook.

"No, her ex-boyfriend Jay bought everything she got on her wrists." Hailey boasted. She stood there very proud.

Cali chuckled. "Yes, he did." Cali agreed.

"What does your ex-boyfriend do?" I probed her for more on her backstory. From the way I stand, she looked like a certified gold digger. The way she carried herself was a dead giveaway.

"He did everything from paying celebrities to come here and perform to buying old houses and flipping them." Cali said confidently. It was very apparent that she wanted me to know that her last boyfriend was a man of status and he was well-known.

"So, what part of Miami are you from?" Cali started questioning me. She seemed like she was dying to ask me that question. So, what was I gonna say? See, now this was why I wanted to go out on the back porch with Nick. To avoid questions like this. And now that I've got my back against the wall, what the hell was I going to do? I can't tell them the truth. I'd be signing my own death certificate if I did. "I'm actually from Georgia. I just live in Miami." I finally answered, but I was lying through my teeth.

"How long have you been living in Miami?" Cali's questions continued.

"Not long. Maybe two years." I lied once more.

"How old are you?" Cali didn't hesitate to ask me.

"I'm in my early thirties," I revealed without giving her my age. The less this chick knew about me the better I felt.

"Have any kids?" She continued while Hailey stood there and listened.

"No," I answered her. "Do you?" I turned the question back on her. I got tired of being grilled by her.

"Nope." She replied quickly and then she fell silent. When I thought she was done asking me questions, she started apologizing to me. "I'm sorry about what happened to your man. Hailey told me that he got shot by a couple of Miami cops."

Taken aback by her statement, anxiety nearly crippled me while I searched my mind for a way not to be offended by Hailey and her nosey ass friend of hers. After five seconds passed, I said, "There's no need to be sorry. Bad things happen all the time and when they do, you got to deal with it and find a way to remedy it."

"Wow! You're so brave. If it were me, I'd be around here popping opioids like my mind was going bad." Cali said. "But thankfully, I'll never have those problems." She added.

"And why not?" I became curious.

"Because I've got two uncles and cousins that are police officers. Everybody in New Orleans knows me." She bragged.

Hearing her say that she was well-known in New Orleans kind of freaked me out, but I remained calm like that confession didn't affect me whatsoever. I did, however, make a mental note that any information I make about me has to be at a minimal. Just in case she wants to make a citizen's arrest.

"Are you okay?" Hailey asked me.

"Yes, I'm fine. Why do you ask?" I asked her.

"I would be in a straight jacket right now if I couldn't have Raymond in my life. And especially now that I'm having his baby." Hailey stated.

"Believe me, it's rough," I told them.

"So, what's going to happen now? Are you going to press charges against the cops that did it?" Cali wanted to know.

I swear when Cali asked me about pursuing the cops that killed, my heart sunk into the pit of my stomach. I became paralyzed. I didn't know what to say. I mean, what was I supposed to say? Say yes? Say no? I'm not sure? But then it came to me, "I can't say what I'm going to do right now. I spoke with his mother right before Nick and I came here. She's pretty much going to handle everything." I finally said, hoping that my answer was good enough to the point that they wouldn't second guess me.

"I don't think that I would've left town. My family and his family would probably be marching around the police station, boycotting their asses." Cali assured Hailey and me both.

"If the shoe was on my foot, I wouldn't be able to rest until those cops pay for what they did to Raymond." Hailey agreed with Cali.

"Can I ask what you do for a living?" Cali asked.

"Yeah, I was going to ask you that too." Hailey joined in.

"I own a beauty salon," I said. The lie rolled off my tongue with ease.

"What's the name of it?" Hailey wanted to know.

"It's called Shear Designs." I continued to lie. Shear Designs was a salon where I got my hair fixed.

"Where is it? Because when I come to visit I'm gonna make sure I come and support you." Cali said.

"Me too. I would love to come and visit after I have this baby." Hailey agreed.

"Near Collins Avenue. I'll give both of y'all the address and stuff before Nick and I leave." I lied once again.

"How do you know Nick? Are you two related?" Cali changed the subject.

"No. We're not blood-related. He and my fiancé were best friends. So, I'm like a sister to him." I told her. I mean, what else was I supposed to say? Tell her that I have like a small crush on him. And the reason why I hadn't acted out on it is because I'm mourning Dylan's death and it wouldn't look right if I fall into Nick's arms, so he could console me? No, she would never be privy to that information.

"Does he have a girlfriend back in Miami?" Cali continued. She wasn't letting up. There was no doubt in my mind that she was interested in getting to know Nick.

"Yeah, I think he's seeing someone," I replied in a way to let her know that he was already taken so back the hell up. But surprisingly, my response didn't stop her in her tracks.

"Well, too bad for her. Because while he's here, I'm gonna be his newfound friend." She said as she smiled deviously, rubbing both of her hands together.

Hailey burst into laughter. "You are such a feisty little thing."

"No, I am not. I just see a good-looking man that I'm interested in getting to know and I if I play my cards right."

"How long ago did you and your ex-boyfriend break up?" I probed her for answers.

"Maybe like five to six months ago." She answered me, looking back at Hailey to help her remember her relationship timeline.

"Yeah, that's about right." Hailey agreed.

"Don't you think it's a little too soon to start seeing someone else?"

"Oh honey, don't worry about me. I can handle myself." Cali said confidently. She wanted me to know with certainty that she was ready for whatever Nick could throw her way. This didn't sit well with me.

"I'm sure you can," I mumbled underneath my voice.

"Did you say something?" Hailey interjected.

"I was talking to myself," I replied nonchalantly.

"You know a lot about Nick, right?" Hailey wondered aloud.

"Yeah, why you ask?"

"Think he and Cali would hit it off?"

"That's a hard question to answer because I don't know Cali on a personal level," I told her.

"Well, tell us about him? What kind of woman does he like? Does he like his women like-skinned or brown skin? Would he date someone with kids? Has he ever said that he wants to get married?" Hailey's questions came one after another.

"Look, all I know is that he's a good guy. He does have a girlfriend back in Miami. But I've never heard him say anything about him wanting to get married." I told them both.

"How does his girlfriend look?" Cali blurted out.

"She's a pretty, light-skin woman with long curly hair. She's a real estate broker and she's one of the best in the business." I said. Everything I had just uttered from my mouth was a pack of lies. Nick has never brought any of his girlfriends around me. He always kept his personal life away from the business life he shared with Dylan. His motto has always been, *never fall in love with a woman, because it would be hard to leave her if the Feds ever came looking to indict him.*

"I betcha' she doesn't look better than my bestie!" Hailey came to Cali's defense.

"That's right bestie! That chick ain't got nothing on me!" Cali said and then they both gave each other a high five.

"Nick doesn't know it but I'm gonna get him to take you out on a date tonight," Hailey suggested.

"That's right best friend! Hook me up!" Cali said cheerfully.

While all of this back and forth shit with Cali and Hailey plotting on Nick, I sat there with my blood boiling on the inside. With all of their giggling and child's play, I decided that it was time for me to get away from them as quickly as I could. So, I stood up from the bar stool and asked them to excuse me because I had to go to the bathroom."

"Okay sure, you know where it is." Hailey assisted me.

"Yes, I do." I sand and thanked her as I made my exit. I couldn't get out of that kitchen quick enough. Those bitches were wearing me down. With all the questions coming at me all at once, I was surprised that I didn't spaz out on their nosy asses.

On my way to the bathroom, I heard whispering but I couldn't make out what they were saying. And I wasn't going to worry about it either. I had bigger fish to fry and throwing a monkey wrench in their plot to get Nick to take Cali out on a date was at the top of my list.

STAYING UNDERNEATH THE RADAR

I had no intentions of using the bathroom. But I went in there anyway, to prevent them from catching me in a lie, just in case they decided that they wanted to walk in this direction of the house. I sat down on the edge of the bathtub with the hopes of trying to figure out how I was going to keep up with all the lies I had just told. It's a known fact that when you tell lies, the truth will eventually come out. And when it does, you will look like a jackass when it's all said and done.

I stayed in the bathroom for about five minutes and then I opened the door quietly so Hailey and Cali wouldn't hear it. Once I was in the hallway, I raced towards the back door that led to the back porch. I refused to be in the company of these women and allow them to trap me for another round of questions. My tolerance level wasn't having it.

Nick and Raymond were laughing when I opened the back door and made my way onto the back porch. After I closed the door I asked them what was so funny?

Nick spoke first. "We're talking about how our grandmother used to whip our asses for taking money from the church collection plates."

I took a seat at the patio table with a huge umbrella shielding us from the sun. The pillow cushions were softer than they looked. "Wait a minute, you two used to steal money from the church's collection plate?"

"Yup, we sure did," Raymond said proudly and then he chuckled.

"That's sad. You guys knew that you were wrong for that." I chastised them.

"Come on Kira, give us a break. We were like 9 and 10 years old." Nick explained.

"Yeah, we were just having fun," Raymond added.

"I bet you were," I told them both, giving them the side eye.

"Hey, there you are." I heard a voice coming from behind me say. I knew it was Hailey without turning around and looking over my shoulders.

"Yeah, why did you leave us?" I heard the other voice say.

"Oh, I'm sorry. I came out here to check on the guys and ended up staying out here." I replied after I slightly turned my body around.

"What are y'all talking about?" Hailey asked as she stepped onto the patio deck and stood next to Raymond.

"We were just telling Kira how Nick and I used to steal money from the church's collection plate."

"I can't believe you're still telling that old story," Hailey commented.

"That's because it's funny. Nick and I had some good times while we were growing up." Raymond continued as he looked over at Nick.

"Yep, we sure did." Nick agreed.

"Oh boy, we don't wanna hear nothing else about when y'all were kids. Now, walk your butt off this patio and pull the fish fryer out of the shed so we can have a fish fry." Hailey instructed him.

"All right, all right. Duty calls." Raymond commented as he walked off the deck.

"You in the mood for some fried fish?" Hailey asked Nick.

"You damn right. I haven't been to a fish fry in a long time." Nick told her.

"Well good because you're gonna enjoy the way Raymond and I fry our fish."

While Raymond grabbed the fry pot from the shed which was only a few yards from the deck, Hailey switched the direction of the conversation. She wanted to know if Nick was seeing someone. I couldn't believe that those words were coming out of her mouth. I had already told her and Cali that Nick was seeing someone? What? She didn't believe me.

"Whatcha' mean seeing someone?" He replied with the silliest facial expression he could muster up. He knew what she meant? And so, did Cali. I sat there and waited for him to answer her.

"If you're asking me if I have a girlfriend, no I don't. But I do have a few female friends I see from time to time." He finally answered her.

Both women looked at me. "I thought you said he had a girlfriend?" Hailey said, directing the question to me.

"I'm sorry. But I thought he did." I managed to say without painting the picture that I knowingly lied to them.

Thankfully Nick came to my rescue. "You must be talking about Shelby." He said to me. "I'm not with her anymore." He continued after he turned his focus back on Hailey and Cali.

"How long were you with her?" Cali didn't hesitate to ask him.

The sound of her voice started irritating the crap out of me. Ugh! I wished she would shut up already. I wanted to tell her to stop being thirty because he doesn't want her.

"Not long." He answered her.

"How long is not long?" she pressed the issue.

"A year maybe."

"Why did y'all break up?" Hailey chimed in.

One by one, they started tag-teaming him. They literally had his back pinned against the wall. And they weren't going to let him breathe until they got all the answers they could get out of him.

"She was one of those jealous types. I couldn't go anywhere without her snapping out on me when she saw how women would look at me."

"Oh see, you wouldn't have that problem out of me. I'm very secure with myself." Cali insisted, her face beamed like a headlight. She acted like she wanted to jump into his arms. But I saw right through her. I knew she was full of bullshit! She was as jealous as the make-believe chick Nick was talking about.

"Since you only have friends, why don't you and Cali get together and go out on a lunch or dinner date?" Hailey suggested.

I can't tell you how hot my blood was boiling in my veins, but I will say that it was hot as fire. I mean, what the hell was Hailey doing? Did she think that it was appropriate for her to play matchmaker in a time like this? Nick and I aren't here on vacation. We're here because we're on the run from the fucking cops.

Before he answered her question, he looked at me. Hailey saw his facial expression and so did Cali. "Whatcha' gotta get permission from Kira?" Hailey asked.

I turned my attention towards Hailey and was three seconds away from cursing her ass out. Why the fuck is she so concerned about why Nick looked at me? She needs to stay in her lane before I rip her ass to shreds. "No, I don't." He told her.

"It looks that way to me," Cali interjected.

"He just values my opinion is all," I spoke up.

"Well then, what's your answer?" Hailey pressed the issue.

"I don't think right now is a good time, especially since I just lost my best friend. I really just wanna hang out around here with my cousin and catch up with him for old times' sake." Nick explained to Cali and Hailey both.

"You sure it's not because of Kira?" Hailey replied sarcastically, but in a jokingly manner. She knew deep down in her heart that I was the reason Nick declined the offer to take Cali out on a date.

"No, it's not because of her."

"Yes, it's not because of me." I blurted out.

"Yeah, whatever." Hailey teased.

"Yo' Nick, come here and help me with this fryer," Raymond yelled from the shed. Raymond stood at the door of the shed with a large, metal pot and the burner that he was going to use to heat up the pot, in his hands.

Without hesitation, Nick got up from the chair and made his way off the patio. I saw the relief in his eyes after Raymond told him that he needed his help. Raymond could not have called him at a better time.

"Don't think you got off the hook," Hailey yelled at him. Nick didn't respond though.

"Have you talked to your fiancé's mother today?" Hailey comes out of nowhere and asked.

"Who me?" I asked her.

"Yes,"

"No, I haven't spoken to her today. Why you asked?" I wanted to know. This bitch was so bold. Who asks questions like that? And why is she always trying to offend me? Do I look like a weak ass bitch to her? Does she get a kick out of asking me personal questions? I know one thing, she better watch her step because I'm very close to disrespecting her nosey ass in her own house.

"I just don't want you to let those cops get away with what they did. I see it on TV every day how cops are getting away with killing our black men." Hailey stated.

"What's your man's name?" Cali chimed in.

Why the fuck does this bitch want to know Dylan's name? We aren't cool like that. And besides, she doesn't even know him, so what is her deal?

"You don't have to tell me if you don't want to." Cali continued.

"Yeah Kira, you don't have to answer if you don't want to," Hailey added.

"Can we just not talk about him at all? When I mourn him, I wanna do it in private." I told them both. But the fact of the matter was that these two women were being intrusive so, I wasn't telling them anything about my life back in Miami. Not now. Not ever.

"Sorry about that," Cali said.

"Yeah, my bad," Hailey replied. But as the seconds turned into minutes, the vibes that loomed over us became really awkward. I couldn't sit there and pretend like everything was okay with these girls, so I stood up from the patio chair and asked the ladies to excuse me. I met Raymond and Nick near the fence, where they were setting up the fish fryer. "Is everything all right? Do you need anything?" Nick asked me.

"No, I'm good. I just wanted to watch you guys while you were setting up the fryer." I lied.

"Kira, this fish is going to be so damn good, you're gonna wanna smack the hell out of this negro after you take the first bite." Raymond chuckled.

"Kira wouldn't do that to me. Right, sis?"

"You got that right." I smiled at them both.

"What were you girls up there talking about?" Raymond wanted to know.

"It seems like Cali has a huge crush on Nick," I spoke up first.

"Word!" Raymond smiled.

"Yep. She asked him if he had a girlfriend." I continued.

"So, she has a crush on you, huh?" Raymond said playfully. "You can't go anywhere without women practically throwing themselves at you," Raymond added.

"I said the same thing." I took Raymond side.

"I betcha' my wife was up there egging that shit on, wasn't she?"

"Yep, she sure was," I assured him.

"I'm gonna tell her about herself later. She's always trying to hook Cali up with every guy I bring over here. She's been out with a couple of my co-workers already but nothing ever comes out of it. They all say that she's a drama queen."

"I can definitely see that," I commented.

"Well, I'm not into drama queens so she can get her eyes off me," Nick announced between us three.

"She's a bit thirsty so it's gonna be entertaining to see how you try to keep her away from you," I added.

"Yeah, I'm with Kira." Raymond chimed in and then he chuckled.

"I can't mess with that chick. I'll have her ass stalking me if she got in bed with me." Nick commented jokingly.

I punched him in his right arm. "Don't play yourself. Stay focused." I instructed him.

Raymond looked at me and Nick both. "Do I detect a little bit of jealousy?"

"No. I just don't want him to lose focus on why we're here in the first place. Cali seems like she's the jealous type and he can't afford to entertain her right now." I explained.

"Yeah, you hit that one out of the park," Raymond told me.

"Let's see if he takes heed to what we are saying," I added.

"Come on now, I'm a grown ass man. Y'all know I can handle myself."

"Nick, I know you know how to handle your business. I'm just saying, Cali, is a handful. So, just think with your head and not with your dick." Raymond warned Nick.

"You ain't gotta worry about that. I've got everything under control." Nick tried to assure us.

"And I'm gonna make sure you stay that way," I interjected.

STICKING & MOVING

I hung out outside with the guys the entire time while Raymond worked the fish fryer. I took the first piece of the catfish after Raymond took it out of the hot grease. I bit into the first bite of the fish and it nearly melted in my mouth. I swear, it was the best freaking fish I had in a very long time. It didn't need any other seasoning nor hot sauce. I've got to remind myself to get another piece for later before they're all gone.

After Raymond turned off the fish fryer and everyone ate, I thanked Raymond for his hospitality and for filling up my belly with his fish and then I excused myself to the guest bedroom so I could get some rest. "I'm gonna take a nap," I told Nick.

"Okay. Cool." He replied and then I headed into the house.

The moment I walked into the house, I heard giggling and whispering coming from Hailey and Raymond's bedroom. I swear, the timing couldn't have been better, because immediately after I had stopped in my tracks, I heard Hailey utter my name. I stood next to the entryway of her bedroom door with hopes of hearing what was being said. "I will bet you money that she's sleeping with Nick." I heard Cali say.

"I don't think she is. From what I hear, her man and Nick were like best friends." Hailey corrected her.

"Well, if they aren't fucking, then something is going on between the two." Cali shot back. She was convinced that something was going on between Nick and me.

"Stop overthinking everything. He's single. You're single so make your move. But wait until you two are alone. If she's lurking somewhere near him, then she will have an effect at how he'll react towards you."

"You could not have said it better." Cali agreed with Hailey. "But let me ask you something," Cali continued.

"What's up?"

"Do you believe that her fiancé was killed by cops?"

"I don't think she'll lie about something like that. And besides, Nick is the one that reached out to Raymond and they're close, so I know he wouldn't lie to his own cousin." Hailey tried to explain.

"Yeah, I guess you're right. But there's just something about her that doesn't seem right."

"What do you think it is?" Hailey seemed interested in Cali's response.

"I don't know."

"Well, don't let it consume you."

Cali chuckled. "Believe me, I won't."

Hailey and Cali continued to talk about me until Hailey suggested that they go back outside. At that moment, I knew that I needed to haul ass to the guest bedroom before they opened the bedroom door and catch me eavesdropping. I know for a fact that that wouldn't go over well with Hailey. It wouldn't go over well with me either if it were my house. So, to keep things civilized, I scurried quietly into the guest bedroom and then I closed the door without making one sound.

I heard Cali and Hailey laughing about something as they passed by the guest bedroom door. The thought of them trying to shade me with their behavior tactics made me upset. How dare they question whether or not Dylan was dead? And why wonder if I'm fucking Nick or not? It's none of their damn business. We are grown women and men, so why don't they act like it? I swear, I want to confront Cali so bad, especially since she's the one asking all the fucking questions. Everything would be all right if she would stay the hell out of my way. I'm not bothering her, so why doesn't she take heed to it?

When the back door to the patio opened and closed, I knew Hailey and Cali had made it outside. I can see it now, as soon as Hailey and Cali see that I am nowhere around, they will corner Nick like a predator dominating their prey. Cali is definitely a thirsty ass tramp. It wouldn't surprise me if she tries to lure Nick into the bathroom and give him a free blow job. That's just how desperate she acts.

My mission for being in this room was so that I could get some me time and reflect on my life. The good. Bad. And the ugly. But as I lay here, I can't seem to get Dylan out of my head. I need him here with me. Not in some fucking coroner's office laying on a cold, metal table. I also couldn't stop thinking about my father. Picturing him burning in that SUV Nick and I left him in suddenly made me sick on my stomach. What kind of daughter was I to do that? Okay, I know I did it to keep Dylan from going to prison but look what good that did? Dylan is dead now. Now I'm without my father and Dylan. What a mess, I've made.

Wallowing in my depressive state of mind, I began to sob. I did my best to muffle my cries but it seemed like the quieter I tried to get, the louder I became. I was hurting so badly and my heart felt so heavy. How was I going to become whole again? Will it ever happen in my lifetime? "Daddy, I'm so sorry, I didn't mean to hurt you. I kept telling you to stop running your mouth to the cops but you wouldn't stop. So, what was I supposed to do? I couldn't let you bring me and Dylan down. That wouldn't have been fair to us. Now look at us, you and Dylan are gone and I'm left here on this earth alone." I cried.

"Kira are you alright?" I heard a voice ask me. Instantly startled by a couple of knocks on the bedroom door, I held my breath and wiped the tears from my face. But it was too late. The person on the other side of the door had already heard me.

I thought for a second, trying to figure out who's voice was on the other side of the door, but my mind wouldn't register it. "Who is it?" I finally got up the gumption to say.

"It's Raymond, can I come in?" He asked. But before I could answer him, he opened the door and walked into the room.

Refusing to let him look at me, I laid my face down on the pillow and had it faced in the opposite of him. The last thing I wanted him to do was to see me crying. Questions would roll in faster than I'd be able to answer. "Are you okay?" He pressed the issue.

"Yes, I'm fine." I lied while trying to speak clearly. I couldn't let him see how upset and sad I was.

"Are you sure? Because I could run out to the backyard and tell Nick to come in here with you." He wouldn't let up. He was hell-bent on getting me to tell him that something was bothering me. But I didn't break.

"I'm good. I just miss my fiancé is all. And right now, I wanna be alone." I told him.

"All right, but if you change your mind. Just let me know."

"Okay," I said.

After Raymond left the bedroom, I laid there quietly, replaying the shootout Dylan and Nick had with the cops and Kendrick's boys. And then I started thinking about Dylan's mother and sister. Everybody is freaking dead. It feels like I'm in the wild, wild west. I can't believe that Nick and I made it out of there without a scratch on us. Was it a blessing in disguise? Or a wake-up call?

MY HEAVY HEART

It didn't surprise me when Nick walked into the bedroom after Raymond left. He knew I was upset so he had to make sure that Nick knew about it. "What's up?" He asked me after sat on the edge of the bed beside me.

By this time, I had covered my face with my right arm, but he moved it out of the way so he could get a better look at me. "Why are you crying?" His questions continued as he started wiping tears away from my eyes and cheeks with his bare hands.

"I'm tired, Nick. I'm tired of living like this." I broke my silence.

"Like what?" He replied as he searched my face for a clearer answer.

"I don't want to be here anymore. I just wanna go back home." I told him as my tears started falling again, this time it felt like the floodgates had opened.

"I understand what you are saying. But you know we can't go back there right now. We're probably on every news station there." He said with certainty.

"Could we just leave from here? Go to a hotel or something?" I pleaded.

"As bad as I want to, it's not safe for us to be at a hotel. What if our pictures have been sent to every news station around the US and someone recognizes us? We'll be in handcuffs and escorted back to Miami quicker than we could blink our eyes."

"So, being here is our only option?" I pressed the issue because I didn't want to be here anymore. I didn't like the vibes coming from Cali and Hailey. They both seemed fake and shady to me.

"Look, I'll tell you what. Let's stay here for a few more days and then if you still feel the same way then I will get Raymond to get a hotel room in his name for us and then we'll leave. Now how does that sound?" He asked me.

I wanted to tell him, no deal, but I felt like what he said was the best decision for us considering our faces could be plastered all over America's Most Wanted. Besides that, Nick was from the streets so he knows how to maneuver in a way to keep the cops off his trail. Whether I wanted to or not, I knew that it was in my best interest to follow Nick's lead, so that's what I intend to do.

Nick sat by my side for a little while until Raymond came knocking on the bedroom door. "Hey Nick, is everything all right?" He yelled from the other side of the door.

Nick got up from the bed and opened the bedroom door. "Yeah, everything is all right. You need me?" Nick replied.

"Nah, I'm just checking on y'all," Raymond told Nick while he looked around the left side of Nick, getting a quick look at me.

"I'm gonna chill in here with Kira for a little while and then I'll come back out there," Nick assured him.

"A'ight. Cool." Raymond said and then he walked away from the door.

Immediately after Nick closed the bedroom down behind Raymond, Nick and I both heard his wife Hailey ask him if everything was all right with me. It sounded like she wasn't standing too far from the bedroom door.

"Yes honey, everything is fine."

"Are you sure? Cali heard her crying earlier." Hailey pressed the issue.

"She misses her fiancé." Raymond reluctantly responded.

I didn't hear Hailey utter another word, so I figured that she went with Raymond's answer and walked away from the door when he did.

"You know everyone is worried about you." Nick insisted.

"Maybe Raymond is but believe me Hailey and Cali isn't." I pointed out.

"Don't say that. Hailey is cool. And so is her friend."

"Cut it out. You know Cali doesn't like me. She wants to fuck you so bad that she can't get her mind straight." I replied sarcastically, but low enough so no one on the other side of the bedroom door could hear me.

"Okay, well maybe she's a little jealous of you because you're getting all of my attention." Nick tried to reason with me while standing over top of me. By this time, he had my full attention too.

"A little jealous? Is that what you call her behavior?"

"Yeah, I guess."

"Well, you're wrong. She's borderline psychotic. I can see right through that bitch! She's a nobody! And I'm telling you right now if you fuck her, she's gonna be a major problem." I said, refusing to hold back any punches.

"You know me well enough to know that I won't let a chick give me problems."

"We're in a different state, so she's a different breed."

"Where's your faith in me?" He asked, giving me a half smile.

"Look, all I want you to do is think twice before you do anything from this day forward. We're on uncharted territory, so there's no room for any hiccups. You understand?"

"Don't worry. I know what I am doing." He insisted.

"I hope so," I replied and then I fell silent.

Of course, Nick wasn't completely sold on the level of confidence I had for him, so he rambled on a little bit more about how he vowed to protect me. He even vowed to never let anyone come between he and I. That part of his vow felt really good to hear. I just hoped that he delivers on it because I have no one else, but him. And whether he believed it or not, I vowed to have his back. I can't go as far as to say that I'd be able to protect him, but I wouldn't let anyone kick him while he's down. That goes for his cousin Raymond and his silly ass wife. If we just stay focused on one another, I believe that he and I will get through this. No if's, and's or but's about it.

CALL WAITING

The guest bedroom that Nick and I shared had a window that gave me a full view of Raymond and Hailey's backyard. So, when I heard laughter and loud dialogue between everyone outside, I got up from the bed and peered out of the window. The first person I saw was Cali laughing and giggling in Nick's face. If he'd give her the okay to kiss him, she would; that was just how close she was to him. Her body language was a tell-all. She continued to lean into him while they stood next to each other on the patio. Hailey and Raymond stood in a huddle with Nick and Cali like they were one big family. The sight of them made me sick to my stomach. Sneaky ass bitches!

While I gritted my teeth at those female vultures, I heard a buzzing sound. I turned away from the window to see where the sound was coming from, but the buzzing stopped. When the buzzing started again, that's when I realized that it was a cell phone. So, I looked down at the floor and underneath the bed but I couldn't find it. I stood still and when I did, I figured out that the buzzing sound from the cell phone was coming from underneath Nick's pillow. I reached under the pillow and grabbed the cell phone. This was Nick's throw-away cell phone, so I wondered who could be calling? I hesitated to answer it, but then I became really curious to see who was on the other end of this call.

Immediately after I pressed the SEND button, I didn't say hello because I wanted the caller to speak first. "Hello," the caller said. It was a woman's voice, so I knew instantly that it was the wrong number. "Hello," I finally replied.

"Who is this?" The woman asked me.

"You called this phone. Now you tell me who you are." I demanded. Why the hell was she calling and answering me who I was? I didn't call her, she called this phone.

"My name is Jennifer and I'm looking for Nick. Is he around?" The woman wanted to know. Shocked by the fact this was a new burner phone, I'm trying to figure out how did she get the number.

"I'm sorry but he's busy right now."

"What do you mean he's busy? You tell him that Jennifer is on the phone and that I need to speak with him." She demanded.

"Look, Jennifer, he's not around." I lied. "So, if you want to talk to him, call him back later."

"So, whatcha' his new girlfriend?"

"No, I am not.

"Then who are you?"

"Let's just say that I am not his girlfriend."

"Are you fucking him?"

"Listen, lady, you're about to be listening to the dial tone if you don't calm your ass down." I snapped. This chick was really getting on my last nerve.

"Who are you talking to like that?" She yelled through the phone.

"Look bitch! Nick can't come to the phone right now. But I will let him know that you called." I said and then I disconnected the call.

My heart was racing uncontrollably. I couldn't believe that I had just had a screaming match with some fucking woman I don't even know. I do know that I need to let Nick know about what had just happened. So, I climbed out of bed and exited the bedroom. When I let myself out of the house and onto the patio, Nick nor Cali was nowhere in sight. The only people present was Raymond and Hailey. They were lounging on their patio furniture when I approached them. "Do you know where Nick is?" I asked Raymond. But Hailey spoke up first.

"Nick took Cali for a walk." She said in a smug manner.

"I thought he walked her to her car?" Raymond said.

"Taking a walk or going to her car is all the same thing," Hailey commented sarcastically.

"Okay, thanks," I replied and headed back into the house. "Fucking bitch!" I mumbled immediately after I closed the patio door.

I marched down the hallway that led to the front of Raymond and Hailey's house. So many thoughts ran through my head as I walked towards the front door. Trying to figure out how I was going to address Nick after I approached him was at the forefront of my mind. I took a deep breath, exhaled and then I opened the front door. To my surprise, Nick and Cali were once again nowhere in sight. I scanned every car window that I could see from where I was standing, but I came up empty. Frustrated and somewhat upset, I slammed the front door closed and headed back in the direction of the back patio. Halfway down the hallway, I heard noise, so I stopped. I stood quietly for a couple of seconds and then I heard the same sound again. I realized then that it was coming from the bathroom, so I tiptoed over to the bathroom door. The sound was faint but I knew it was coming from a man. Without much thought, I knocked on the door. Boom!

Boom! Boom! "Nick are you in there?" I yelled through the door.

"Yeah, what's up? You need something?" He asked me. It sounded like he was rustling around. There was a lot of physical movement.

"Are you using the bathroom?"

"Give me a minute. I'll be out in a second."

"Okay," I said and then I walked away from the door. I didn't walk far though. I stood about ten feet away from the entryway of the bathroom door. This gave Nick enough room to exit the bathroom, but it also gave me a lot of room to investigate things from a safe distance.

After rummaging around in the bathroom for at least another minute, Nick finally opened the door, walked out into the hallway and closed it behind him. He had a guilty expression on his face when he began to walk towards me. "What's up?" He said. I could tell that he was trying to figure out what mood I was in, so I played his game with him. He was giving off the vibe that, *if I don't ask, then he won't tell*.

"Where's Cali?" I didn't hesitate to ask. I wasted no time in putting him in the hot seat.

"Why? What's wrong?" He asked me. I knew he was trying to be evasive.

"Raymond and Hailey told me that you and her were taking a walk outside somewhere," I replied, watching his body language because something was telling me that Cali was in that damn bathroom. "So, where is she?" I pressed him.

"I'm right here." I heard a woman's voice say as the bathroom door slowly opened. I peered over Nick's shoulders and my poor heart nearly leaped out of my chest when I saw Cali walking out of the bathroom the same way Nick did. So many thoughts were circulating in my head that I couldn't think straight. One part of me wanted to rip her hair from her head while the other part wanted me to do the same to Nick. So, before I could figure out what my next course of action would be, Cali walked towards me and asked me what was my deal and why was I so concerned about where she was?

I swear after she said that, I lost all of my composure. "What's my deal?" I repeated.

"Yeah, what's up with you?" She replied in a snide manner.

"First of all, I know you're a ho! And I know that you're looking for a come up. You figure that if you give Nick some pussy and give it to him right, then he'll buy you something nice and expensive. And who knows, he may even ask you to be his woman. But let me be the first to tell you that, that ain't gonna happen because he's used to dealing with cunts like you. He knows a slut when he sees one."

"It takes one to know one!" Cali shot back at me.

"Bitch, I'm not the one with cum all around my mouth. I know you were in there sucking his dick."

"Come on now Kira, let's not do that." Nick tried defusing the situation. But I refused to listen to him. She had pressed my last button.

"Why are you so jealous of me?" She asked me.

"Jealous? Jealous of what? You're a troll looking for a come up. But Nick ain't into taking care of hos like you. He likes classy chicks." I spat.

"I suppose that you're the classy chick, huh?" She chuckled.

"You damn right!" I replied confidently.

"I'm sorry, but you're not acting classy now," Cali replied sarcastically, giving me a smirk like expression.

"You think you're funny, huh?!"

"I'm not the one acting like a clown!" She said nonchalantly, standing before me with that same smirk on her face.

"Nick you better get this bitch before I go off on her ass!" I warned Nick.

"Come on Cali, let's go back to the patio." Nick grabbed her arm and tried to escort her in the opposite direction.

"Yes, get that ho away from me before I go ham on her silly ass!" I snapped.

"What's going on?" I heard Hailey say after the patio door closed.

"Yeah, what's going on in here?" Raymond chimed in.

"This jealous ass bitch is in here talking smack because Nick and I were spending time together in the bathroom," Cali spoke up first.

"Nah, tell her the truth. Tell her you were in the bathroom sucking Nick's dick and I interrupted you." I blurted out. I wanted Hailey and Raymond to know the truth.

"So, what? Why are you so concerned about what she does with her mouth?" Hailey interjected. She made it perfectly clear that she was on Cali's side and it didn't surprise me. But what did surprise me was that Hailey wasn't embarrassed that her BFF was sucking a complete stranger's dick in her house. Who does that?

"So, it's okay for her to suck the dick of a man she just met like a couple of hours ago? And she did it in your house too." I asked with extreme sarcasm.

"The last time I checked, she was a grown ass woman." Hailey shot back.

"You know they say, the apple doesn't fall too far from the tree." I pointed out, with another level of sarcasm.

"Oh so, now you're saying that I'll do something like that because my best friend did it?" Hailey wanted to know. She was testing me.

"Bingo!" I blurted.

"Hailey, this bitch is really bold!" Cali instigated from sidelines.

"Stop it, Cali! Enough with all this shit!" Raymond roared.

"Kira, let's go in the room so you can calm down." Nick insisted and tried to pull me in the direction of the guest bedroom.

"I'm sorry Nick but she ain't staying in here. She gotta go." Hailey told him.

"And where is she gonna go?" Raymond wanted to know.

"Yeah Hailey, let's not make any irrational decisions right now. I know everybody is upset right now, but if we all sit down like adults, I know we can come to a reasonable solution." Nick stated.

"Nah Nick, we ain't gotta do all of that. I told you yesterday that coming here wasn't going to be a good idea."

Great! So, it's settled. Let her get her shit and get out of here." Hailey added.

I stormed off towards the guest bedroom and Nick followed. "Come on Kira, we can work this out." Nick tried to reason with me.

"Hailey why you gotta be so damn controlling all the time. Give her a break! She's going through something right now." I heard Raymond say.

"So, it's okay for her to disrespect me?"

"Yeah, that bitch is real disrespectful Raymond," Cali interjected.

"If you weren't in the bathroom sucking my cousin's dick then none of this would be happening." Raymond roared.

"I'm grown so I can suck whoever's dick I want to." Cali defended herself.

"See that's the problem. If you would stop being a ho and allowing dudes to play you, then you'd probably have a man by now." Raymond added. "None of the dudes I know don't wanna wife you up because they know what type of chick you are." He continued.

"Don't talk to her like that." Hailey tried to defend her friend.

"Fuck your friend." Raymond roared again and then I heard him storm off. He didn't come to the guest bedroom, so I guess he went to another part of the house.

After Raymond left them, I could hear Hailey and Cali talking about me. They purposely talked loud so that I could hear what they were saying. They were saying everything from how boogie I was to how they know that I'm either fucking Nick or that I'm extremely jealous because they were more attractive than I was. Now that was some serious bullshit to hear, especially since I wasn't able to defend myself. Nick stopped me twice from leaving out of the guest bedroom so that I could confront them. "So, you're gonna let them stand out there and talk about me like that?" I argued.

"Kira, fuck them! Let them talk! They wished that they were half the woman you are?"

"All of this is your fault! You told me that you weren't going to fuck with that nasty ass slut! But you did it anyway." I chastised him, while I began to pack my clothes.

"Kira, whatcha' want me to say? I'm a man with needs."

"So, because you got needs, you go in the bathroom and let that bitch suck your dick?!" I snapped on him. I was so freaking upset with him. Even though Nick and I weren't romantically involved, I felt like he disrespected me.

"I'm sorry you feel that way." He replied as he sat on the edge of the bed a few inches away from me.

"It's too late for that. Just pack up your stuff so we can get out of here before I kill one of those bitches in there." I encouraged him.

"You know it's not a good idea for us to leave." He stated in a low volume.

"Is that why you're not packing your stuff?"

"If I can get Hailey to let us stay here, will you apologize to her?"

Taken aback by Nick's outlandish proposal, I looked at him like he lost his damn mind. "Are you serious right now?"

"Listen, I know you said some words to her and she said some to you, but at the end of the day, we gotta be able to apologize to one another and move past it. It's that simple." Nick tried to reason with me. But I wasn't feeling him or anything he was saying. I was ready to leave this fucking house now and there was nothing anyone could do or say to make me change my mind.

"Let me make one thing clear, I'm not apologizing to her. She stuck her mouth in a conversation Cali and I was having. Not the other way around."

"I understand all of that Kira. But we're in her house, so she felt like you disrespected her."

"You can talk until your head falls off. I am not saying shit to that stupid bitch! I'm packing up all my things and I'm getting out of here."

Instead of trying to convince me to tell Hailey sorry, Nick got up from the bed and walked out of the room. I had no idea what he was going to do, and at this point, I really didn't care. I was leaving this fucking place and that was final.

DRAMA FREE ZONE

After I gathered my belongings, I headed to the front door. Hailey and Cali were sitting at the kitchen table when I walked by. I heard Hailey mumble something and Cali burst into laughter. "If I were you, I wouldn't be laughing, because I know your breath gotta' be reeking from Nick's semen," I said calmly and then I winked my eye at her.

"Whatcha' mad because he won't let you suck his dick?" Cali stood up from the chair and said.

"I don't know why you're getting out the chair, because you ain't gonna do shit but stand there and run your fucking mouth." I challenged her.

"I thought you said that you were classy? You don't like you're being classy now!" Cali mocked me.

"Get out of my house right now!" Hailey shouted at me and then she stood up from the chair.

The second Raymond and Nick heard Hailey shouting they rushed in from the back patio. "What's going on now?" Raymond spoke up first.

I stood at the front door with my blood boiling on the inside. I was on the verge of knocking over lamps and the sofa chairs in the living room but I decided against it when Nick started walking towards me.

"Get that bitch out of my house right now!" Hailey threatened.

"What just happened?" Nick asked me.

"I was standing here waiting on you so we can leave and they started running their mouths," I explained.

"Nick, you better get her out of my house before I call the police," Hailey warned him.

"You're not calling the fucking police on them. So, stop it." Raymond shouted at Hailey. I could tell that he was as upset by this whole thing than I was.

"Who's gonna stop me, you?" She said and then I heard some rumbling in the kitchen. "Raymond, move out of my way," Hailey demanded.

"No, I'm not going anywhere so have a seat," Raymond instructed her.

"I need you to go in the room and get your things because I am ready to go," I told Nick while Raymond was in the kitchen trying to convince Hailey to calm down.

"But Raymond and I were talking…." Nick began to say but I cut him off in mid-sentence.

"Look, I don't wanna hear anything about what you and Raymond were talking about. I am ready to go." I told him as I stood my ground.

"Nick, you can stay but she's got to go," Hailey yelled from the kitchen.

"Bitch, you gotta be crazy if you think that he's going stay here while I leave," I yelled back at her.

"Who are you calling a bitch?" Hailey roared. I heard the barstool being pushed across the floor.

"I'm calling you one, bitch!" I shouted back.

"Now, see I'm getting tired of hearing this ho's mouth!" I heard Cali say and then I heard footsteps scurrying across the kitchen. I had no idea she was charging at me until I saw her coming around the corner through my peripheral vision. When she got within arms reach of Nick and me, she lunged back and threw her first punch. I ducked just in time, but Nick was hit in the back of his head. "What the fuck!" Nick roared after the blow hit him. From there, everything fell apart. "This bitch really tried to hit me," I said and lunged my purse back her. I managed to strike her in the face with it. Then I lunged it at her again, hitting her arms because she was using them to shield her head.

While Nick was trying to stop me from hitting Cali with my purse Hailey came from out of nowhere and snatched my purse from the grips of my hand. And before I knew it, she was hitting me with my own handbag. "You dumb bitch! How does it feel to be hit in your fucking head?!" Hailey roared.

"Hailey, stop! What the fuck are you doing?!" I heard Raymond shouting.

"Yeah Hailey, get that bitch!" Cali spat while Nick had her penned in a corner near the front door.

"Yeah Hailey, come and get me!" I dared her while I jumped around, ducking every blow she threw at me.

"Raymond, will you please get her!" Nick instructed him.

"Nah Raymond, don't get her because if she hits me, I'm gonna make her have her baby real early," I warned Raymond.

"Why don't you hit me since you're so fucking bad!" Hailey dared me, swinging my purse at me every chance she got.

I got tired of jumping and hopping around in this living room so gritted my teeth and snatched my purse back out of her hands. And when I swung it at her, she managed to duck it. Raymond didn't like this. "You trying to hit my wife?" He roared and then he rushed towards me.

Nick saw this and went bananas. "You're trying to hit my wife?!" He spat and stood between Hailey and me and got in my face.

"She tried to hit me first." I protested, raising my voice to get my point across.

"Get out! Get out of my house!" Raymond shouted at me.

"Fuck y'all!" I hissed at everyone in the room. Then I looked at Nick and said, "Let's go." Seconds later, I was on walking off Raymond and Hailey's front porch and walking towards Nick's truck.

Trembling from the rage brewing inside of me, I found myself trying to cope with the fact that things between Nick's family and I are on the outs and there wasn't any going back. I was officially on their shit list and I could honestly care less.

Like I mentioned before, I knew that I wasn't going to like being here. I guess my intuition was spot on. I do, however, hope that I haven't caused any bad blood between Nick and Raymond. Being around those two while they caught up on old times, I could genuinely tell that they love and really missed each other over the years. And because of that, I hope things don't go south between those two.

Since I didn't have the keys to his truck I had to stand there and wait for him to come out of the house. While I stood there livid about what had just gone down back in the house, I broke down in tears. Heartbroken about everything that's been going on, one after another, was consuming me. On the run from the cops, just got into a fighting match with Nick's family and because of it, I'm out on the street. What else can go wrong?

"Are you all right ma'am?" I heard a male's voice say. I was caught off guard, so when I turned around and realized that a black, uninformed, New Orleans' cop was talking to me, my knees started buckling underneath me. I knew I had to remain calm and not draw more attention to me than I already had, or face the chances of this cop running my name in the law enforcement's database and finding out that I was on the run.

"Yes, I'm fine officer." I managed to say.

"What's your name?" He wanted to know.

Panic-stricken, my heart rate sped up to an uncontrollable speed and my mind went blank. Everything around me disappeared. If felt like it was just me and this cop on this street all by ourselves. So, what was I to do? What had I done wrong for him to ask me what my name was? Had he recognized me? "Kimberly," I finally said. That was the first name that popped up in my head.

"Kimberly what?" He pressed me.

"Kimberly Rawlins," I told him. I swear, if this cop asks me another question about who I was, I'm gonna sprint down the street like Flo Jo.

"Come here and let me get a better look at you." He wouldn't let up. This fucking cop is on to me. So, what am I going to do? I was about to take off and leave my bags behind but what if I get caught? This situation for me to end all wrong and I can't let that happen.

Terrified about what was going to happen next, I walked over to the cop's car as slowly as I could. As I approached him, he turned on the interior light of his patrol car, I'm guessing to get a better look at me. *Please God, don't let this police officer recognize me. Not now. Not here. I promise I will do what you ask God!*

When I finally approached the passenger side door of the officer's car, he picked up his flashlight and shined it on me. I squinted my eyes and shield half of my face with my hand. "You're not from around, here are you?" He didn't hesitate to ask.

"No, I'm not. My husband and I are here visiting relatives. It's the house next to this one we're standing in front of." I managed to lie and say. "There names are Raymond and Hailey. Hailey's my sister-in-law. She's pregnant with their first child. So, we're here to attend their baby shower." I added. I tried to sound as convincing as I could.

"Well, you be careful around here. This city has it's fair share of criminals running around here looking to find something to get into. So, if you're getting ready to get in that truck to leave, then I encourage you to do so."

"Don't worry. My husband is in the house grabbing his keys right now." I told him.

"All right, well take it easy."

"I will. And thanks again." I said and then I watched him as he drove away. "Oh my God! Where the fuck did he just come from?" I mumbled to myself, heart still racing one hundred miles per second. If he was a white police officer, he might've pulled to the side of the street and started harassing me. Thank God that that didn't happen.

I knew standing outside in the opening was too risky so I started walking back towards Raymond's house so I could encourage Nick to hurry up. Fortunately for me, he and Raymond were standing on the porch talking when I approached the house. I let out a loud sigh and asked him politely if he could come on so we could leave.

"I'm coming." He replied and then a few seconds later, he began to head my way and Raymond followed.

Before Nick and Raymond could get down the stairs good, the front to the house opened and Hailey stood there in the doorway with a few words to say. "Where are you going?" I heard her ask.

"I'm showing Nick where the hotels are around here," Raymond told her.

"He has a GPS. Let 'em find it himself." She argued.

"Just go in the house until I come back," Raymond instructed her.

"If you leave and go with them, then you're not coming back in this house." Hailey threatens him.

"Go back in the house Hailey. Don't make a scene." Raymond yelled back at her.

"I'm not going anywhere until you come back into this house." She roared. She was livid by the fact that Raymond was helping Nick find a hotel, especially after the big fight we all had. She probably feels like Raymond is betraying her. In a sense, I feel the same way too. The fact that I know now that Nick allowed Cali to sick his dick in the bathroom, makes me look at Nick in an entirely different way. To let a bad judgment call like that interfere with the real reason why we are here has me concerned about whether or not I can continue to trust him with my life. We are on the run for our lives. So, we have no time nor room for any errors on our part. We don't need

117

anything clouding our judgment. If I want to die or get caught, I'd let Kendrick kill me or turned myself in and told homicide detectives that I had something to do with my father's death and his judge friend and the wife. It would've been as simple as that. I could've stayed in Miami if I wanted to go through all of this unnecessary drama.

"Come on, let's go," Nick said to me after he met me in the middle of the sidewalk. So, I immediately turned around and followed him back to his truck, while Raymond crawled inside of his car.

"You ain't nothing but a fucking trader!"

"Go inside the house Hailey." He yelled before he closed his car door.

"Fuck you! I'm not going anywhere until you come back into this house." She added, but he started the ignition to his car and couldn't hear her over the engine.

"Bitches like you sure know how to mess up a happy home!" I heard her yell at me.

"If I had to come here all the way from Miami to mess up your happy home, then it wasn't that happy, to begin with," I yelled back at her, not once turning around to face her. I heard her say something to the contrary of me being a phony bitch and that I was going to regret ever coming into her home and disrespecting her. I ignored her and climbed into

Nick's truck. We kept the windows rolled up so we wouldn't hear another word that tramp had to say while we were driving away.

"You will not believe what just happened to me." I started the conversation.

"What happened?"

"While I was standing next to your truck, waiting for you to come outside, a freaking cop drove up and asked me for my name. I swear, I thought he knew who I was and was going to arrest me. I think by me telling him that I was married and that I was from out of town, and here visiting our in-laws for a baby shower, he let me go."

"Was he black or white?"

"He was black. And he scared the shit out of me too. There was no doubt in my mind that I wasn't going to jail tonight. For a moment, I thought that he knew who I was." I said with certainty.

"Thank God he didn't," Nick replied.

"You telling me." I agreed.

"We can't let that happen anymore. No more walking off by yourself."

"You don't have to tell me twice," I assured him.

WHERE TO NEXT?

Nick followed Raymond down a half a block to a stop sign. He signaled for Nick to pull his truck along with his car. Immediately after their vehicles were side by side, Raymond instructed Nick to follow him down to Felicity Street. He told Nick and me that the hotels in that area aren't as popular as the hotels near the French Quarters and Bourbon Street. I was somewhat relieved by Raymond's statement, but I didn't tell him that. I did, however, thank him for coming out to help Nick and I find a hotel. "What's you guys budget for the hotel?" Raymond asked from his car.

I spoke up first. "I don't care how much it costs. But it has to be a four to a five-star hotel. And I don't do old blankets and bed bugs."

"When then, follow me." He told us and sped off.

Raymond pulled out into the road that eventually led to the nearest highway and we followed. The drive started off quiet but there was awkwardness looming in the car so I had no other choice but to address what happened back at Raymond's home. "I'm sorry about what happened back at Raymond's place." I started off.

"Don't even worry about. What's done is done."

"Think Raymond would've hit me if I had hit Hailey with my purse?"

"I don't know what that dude would've done. But I do know that he's tired of her ass. While we were on the porch talking, he told me that he blames her and Cali for picking that fight with you. He said that he was going to tell you that he's sorry for it too."

"Really? He said that?"

"Yeah, I guess the happy marriage I told you about isn't happy at all."

"Well, I'm glad he realized that I wasn't trying to be messy."

"It was relieved by that too."

"I know she probably hates my guts."

"Oh, it's worse than that. You should've heard her talking about you while I was still in the house."

"I can imagine." I started off and then I said, "Oh and I bet her friend Cali had a lot to say about me too."

"Yeah, she was running her mouth too. But it's only because they're jealous of you. I mean, look how beautiful you are. You see how Raymond reacted when he first saw you. He was smiling from ear to ear." Nick pointed out.

"Yes, I saw that. But did you see how Hailey reacted when she saw how eager he was to get me something to drink from the refrigerator."

"Yes, she was pissed."

"Well, there you go." He said, not taking his eyes off the traffic in front of us.

I believe we drove ten miles away from Raymond's home. We pulled into the parking lot of a Dresco Inn. Nick and I stayed in the car until Raymond booked our room and paid for it. Immediately after he gave Nick the key he apologized again for Hailey's actions back at the house. Nick assured him at least four times that everything was cool, even though I knew it was the opposite. "Call me later if you need something," Raymond told him.

"I will. And thanks again." Nick replied.

While I watched Raymond leave the parking lot of the hotel, Nick drove his car to the other side of the motel, because that was where our room was located. It was on the 2nd floor too, which was also good. "Being on the second floor will allow us to see whosever coming." He acknowledged.

I smiled at him. "Great minds think alike," I commented.

"Let's get our bags and head up to our room."

"Copy that," I said and grabbed my things from the back seat.

We didn't have a lot of baggage, so we were out of the car and inside our 3-and-a-half-star motel with one trip. "Ewwww... do you smell that?" I asked Nick after he opened the door and I walked in.

"Yeah, it smells like mothballs and Benjay," Nick commented.

"I swear, if I had a choice about where we were going to say, we wouldn't be here. And since I am the reason why we got kicked out of Raymond and Hailey's home, I'm gonna suck this one up and deal with it.

After Nick and I got settled, he started watching television and I started thinking about the call that came through on the burner phone. Nick was sitting at the small table near the door of the room when I brought the subject up. "Some rude chick name Jennifer called the burner phone," I mentioned and then I slid off the bed and handed him the throwaway cell phone.

"When did this happen?" He wanted to know after taking the phone into his hand.

"Right when I found Cali in the bathroom sucking on your dick," I replied sarcastically.

"Why was she rude? What did she say?"

"She asked me if she could speak to you. I told her that you were busy and got smart with me."

"Was that all she said?" He pressed the issue.

"Look, she wanted to know if I was fucking you. So, I told her no. Then one question led to another. She was really tripping out. In the end, I got her ass off the phone and that's all that matters, right?"

"Right," Nick replied while he looked at the phone number in the call log.

"I thought that was one of your throwaway phones."

"It is."

"So, how did she get the number?"

"See, Jennifer was a chick I'll kick it with from time to time. She would go and run errands for me and I'll hit her off with a few hundred dollars. So, the night before Kendrick and boys kidnapped you, I got her to run by the corner store and grab me three phones. Now, the only way she could've gotten the number to this phone is if she took it from the card that was inside the package."

"Well, there you go," I replied sarcastically.

"I wonder if she got the numbers to those other throwaways?" Nick asked out loud.

"It's a possibility." I let him know. "So, what are you going to do?" I continued to question him.

"I don't know."

124

"I think you should call her back. She called you for a reason."

"What if she's trying to set me up?"

"What if she isn't?"

"I can't chance it," Nick concluded and then he powered the cell phone off. Immediately after, he placed the phone on the floor and stomped on it. He crushed it into three pieces. When he picked up the pieces from the floor, he discarded them into the kitchen trash can.

"So, what are you going to do now?" I wondered aloud. I wanted to know what his next plan was.

"I'm sorting that out in my head right now."

"Are you ever going back over to Raymond's place?"

"Why you ask?"

"I'm just curious."

"To answer your question, I really don't know. I mean, he is my family and I really wanna spend time with him. But, knowing how things ended with you and his wife, I don't think it would be a good idea if I went."

"I really appreciate what you're saying. But, it's been years since you seen him, so I wouldn't mind if you go back over there and spend time with him, just as long as you don't end back up in the bathroom and let Cali suck on your dick again."

"You're really upset about, huh?"

"Yes, I am."

"Why?"

"Because you don't need the distraction. And besides, she's a ho! You know that you could still contract herpes from getting head?"

"Yes, I know. But tell me the real reason why you were upset? I feel like you're trying to hold something back from me."

"Nick, what do you want me to say?"

"I want you to tell me the truth."

"I already told you the truth."

"Kira, why don't you tell me how much you really care about me?"

Shocked by Nick's question, my heart dropped into the pit of my stomach. I couldn't believe how he was on to me. "There's nothing to say. You already know that I love you as a brother."

"Stop it, Kira! I know you love me. Because if you didn't, you wouldn't act the way you do when I'm around other women. And it's okay because I love you too. I fell in love with you the night I helped you get rid of your father. It felt like we could conquer the world. We were a modern day Bonnie and Clyde. What I did for you, I'd never do it for another woman."

My heart fluttered when Nick acknowledged that he knew that I loved him. It was almost unbelievable to hear him say it. "You know that this isn't right." I began to say, but my heart was saying the total opposite.

"I know it isn't. But I can't seem to get the feelings I have for you out of my heart." He added.

I looked away from him and turned my attention towards the TV. I figured if I do this, I'll be able to control my emotions. Hold back the feelings that were brewing inside of me. For one, it was wrong. I was engaged to Dylan before he was killed. And he and Dylan were like brothers. So, how would this look to people that knew the history of me, Dylan and Nick? I would be called a ho quicker than I could blink my eyes and I can't have that.

"Do you love me?" He pressed me. He wasn't letting me off the hook.

"I can't answer that," I replied, trying my best to avoid looking at him straight on. He wasn't having it and grabbed the bottom of my chin and slowly turned my face around to face him.

"It's okay to love me, Kira. Because I'm in love with you." He stated, looking me directly in the eyes. The flutters in my heart became more intense. I swear, I've never felt love like this before. And all I wanted Nick to do right now is hold me in his arms.

"Will you hold me?" I asked him, my voice cracking while my eyes filled with water.

"I thought you'd never ask." He said and pulled me up from the bed. He held on me so tight and I didn't want him to let me go.

While he was holding me in my arms, my tears started falling from my eyes. "It's okay to cry." He told me.

"What are people gonna say about us?" I sobbed over his shoulders.

"I don't care what they say. I'm in love with you and I'm gonna take care of you." "Do you promise to never hurt me?"

He backed away from me so he could get a look at my face. "I promise I will never hurt you. I'm gonna love you more and more with each passing day." He said and grabbed my face and brought it close to his. Next, I closed my eyes. When our lips locked, it felt like magic. Fireworks were going off inside of me and it felt good when he placed his sweet tasting lips on top of mine and we began kissing passionately. He tasted so good. I could feel myself growing hot and my pussy getting wet. He moved in closer and pushed me back on the bed. Then he climbed on top of me. I could feel his dick hard against my pelvis. His hands started traveling to different places on my body and that made me feel like I was on cloud nine so I began grinding my hips upward towards his dick trying to press my clit on his rock-hard shit. I wanted him to know that I wanted to feel him inside of me real bad. He lifted my shirt and with one touch he had the front clasp on my bra loosened. My size D cup breasts jumped loose and Duke put his mouth on my nipples. "Ohhh," I sang out. The heat from his mouth was sending me over the top. He sucked on my nipples so hard he caused me to grind harder and faster. It felt so good I had to move my head side-to-side. Each time I moved, Nick sucked harder and harder. I couldn't control myself.

"I want you!" I screamed out.

My pussy was soaking wet. I could feel the moisture in my panties. He stood back up abruptly and hovered over me. I looked up at him with innocent eyes. He quickly unbuttoned my jean shorts and pulled them down over my hips and all the way off. The cool air on my clit made me feel hot as hell. I spread my legs open so he could get a good look at my creamy pussy. Any inhibitions I had previously had about sleeping with him early were gone.

"Damn, that is a pretty pussy! Mmmm, mmm," he complimented. I reached down and put my index finger in my pussy. I fingered my pussy, sliding my finger in and out, enticing him.

"Shit!" he moaned, grabbing his dick through his pants. Then he did some shit that surprised me. He dropped to his knees in front of me and put his face between my legs.

"Ahhh," I screamed out. Nick started darting his tongue into my hole real fast, in and out. "Oh God! Oh God! Oh God!" I hollered. My moans just drove him crazier. He made loud slurping noises while he ate the shit out of my pussy. I was pumping my ass, shoving that pussy at his tongue.

"C'mon . . . give it to me," I told him. He got up and slid out of his jeans. His legs were so toned and his dick hung almost to his knees. I licked my lips but before I could go down on him, Nick hoisted me up and held me against him. I put my legs up around his waist and straddled him. I held onto his neck so I wouldn't fall while he guided his dick into my pussy.

"Owww!" I screamed when he put his thick, solid dick into me. He flopped back on the couch and now I was riding him. I bounced up and down on that dick so hard and fast he was breathing like he had just run laps. "Oh, fuck me! Fuck me good," I talked much shit while I rode that dick.

"Oh shit, girl, your pussy is out of this fucking world," he growled. Just when I thought he was going to cum, I jumped up off his dick and then I turned around and got back on his dick backwards so he could see my whole ass, *the reverse cowgirl*. No man worth his salt could turn this shit down. Seeing a woman in this position made men's dicks harder and added to the throbbing sensation.

I bent over at the waist and pumped up and down on his dick again. "Awww fuck!" he moaned. Nick slapped my ass cheeks as I fucked the shit out of him. I planted my feet for leverage and then I used both of my hands and spread my ass cheeks apart so he could see his dick go in and out of my pussy. "I see it! Fuck me! I see it!" Nick called out. This was what us women live for—to drive a muthafucka crazy tapping that ass. The ultimate in pussy whipping.

I started to feel myself about to cum because the shaft of his dick was pressing on my g-spot. "I'm coming!" I called out and then I sat up, closed my legs together and squeezed his dick with my pussy.

"Agggghhhh!" Nick bucked and screamed. He was coming as well. I jumped up quickly but I think some of his cum had got inside of me. I turned around and he started jerking the rest of his cum onto my tits. That turned him on even more. "Goddamn girl, that was some bomb ass pussy," he gasped. He started rubbing his dick and I watched it start to grow hard again.

"C'mere . . . where you going?" he asked me, trying to pull me back down on the bed.

I chuckled like a little school girl. "To the bathroom," I told him.

"I now see why Dylan loved you so much." He commented.

I just stood there and looked at Nick, wondering what Dylan would do if he caught us in this hotel room together. "Why?" I got up the gumption to say.

"I can think of a lot of reasons. But the main one that sticks out is that you're the whole package. You're beautiful. You're smart. And you're easy to love. You're an overall sweetheart!"

I blushed. Hearing all those compliments gave me a huge ego boost for me, considering he's been with a lot of women. So, did I make the right decision to have sex with Nick? Or was I going to regret it? I guess time will tell.

A NEW DAY

I slept like a baby last night. But when I woke this morning and found out that Nick wasn't in the bed with me, I got a little concerned. I couldn't call him because I didn't know the number of the other burner cell phones that he had. All I could do was wait.

After sitting around in the hotel room for close to an hour, Nick finally walked back into the room bearing cups of Cappuccinos and Beignets with a mountain of powdered sugar on top of them. I stormed towards him and punched him in his right arm after he sat the food down on the table holding the TV. "Owww, what was that for?" He whined and started massaging his arm.

"I was scared out of my mind when I woke up and realized that you were gone."

"I only went to get us something to eat."

"You should've woken me up and told me."

"I wanted to but you looked so peaceful in your sleep."

"I don't wanna hear that, Nick. Just tell me that you won't do that again."

"I promise that I won't ever do it again." He said and then he smiled at me.

"You better not." I dared him and then I sat down in one of the chairs placed at the small table near the hotel room door.

"I got a call from Raymond while I was out." He changed the subject and as he walked towards me with a cup of the Cappuccino and a Beignet wrapped in a napkin.

"What did he say?" I asked after I took the coffee and pastry from his hand.

"I didn't tell you this before, but he owes me money. So, the real reason I am here is because I'm trying to collect on it."

"How much does he owe you?"

"Twenty grand. I lent him that money a little over a year ago so he could make the down payment on the house he lives in today."

"But, I thought that you two hadn't seen each other in years."

"We haven't."

"So, how did he get the money?"

"I got that girl Jennifer to wire him the dough when he called me and asked for it."

"That chick Jennifer sure does a lot of your dirty work, huh?"

"Yeah, she's done a few things here and there for me."

"Well, as of today that stops, right?"

"Of course, it does. What do I need her for when I have you now?" Nick blushed.

"Yeah, and it better stay that way too." I gave him a smirk. And then I switched the conversation back to Raymond and the money he owes Nick. "So, did he say he has the money?" I wanted to know. I mean, who has that type of money around?

"When we talked about it yesterday, he told me to give him a couple of days and he'll be able to get it."

"Do you believe him?"

"Do I have any other choice? I mean, we need money really bad. That three grand I scrambled up from my apartment isn't going to last us very long. At least with the twenty grand, I'll be able to make some moves and stretch the money out a little bit more."

"What kind of moves?"

"Remember when Raymond came outside and got me after he heard you crying?"

"Yes,"

"I was in the middle of a conversation with a major connect that Dylan and I have out in LA. I was introduced to the connect by Dylan. Dylan did a couple of murder-for-hire jobs for them and he won their trust by doing it. So, I told 'em that Dylan and I had a run in with some cats in Miami and as the result of that, Dylan was killed. And then I told 'em that I had you with me and as soon as I said that, they told me to come out there and they will take care of us. So, as soon as I get this money from Raymond, we're gonna bounce."

"What if Raymond doesn't come up with it?" I asked him. I needed for him to know that there's a chance that Raymond may not be able to come up with that kind of money. If he could, then he wouldn't have called Nick a year ago and ask him for it.

"I can't even wrap my head around that right now. So, let's try to be optimistic." Nick said as he grabbed his cup of coffee and a Beignet for himself. He sat down on the next across from me and took a bite of his pastry.

"As you wish," I replied and then I took a sip of my Cappuccino.

"Do you know that you've made me the happiest man in the world?"

"And when did I do that?"

"Just being here with me. The way you make me feel being able to share this space with you. Kira, you mean the world to me. And I'm more in love with you today than I was last night. I've never been in love like this before. So, I will never let anyone come between that."

Hearing Nick once again, proclaiming his love for me made my heart flicker all over again. Falling deeper in love for this man was definitely on the horizon for me. For the first time in my life, I feel like I could trust a man 100%. This was a good thing and I look forward to going on this journey with him. "I will never let anyone come between you and me either," I assured him and then I leaned over the table and kissed him in the mouth. After I sat back down in my chair, I asked him what time was he leaving.

"After I get out of the shower." He told me.

"How long are you going to be?"

"Not long. We probably take a drive somewhere. So, maybe an hour or two."

"Just make sure you be careful. That cop that stopped me last night said that there's a lot of criminals in that area." I reminded him.

"Yeah, I know. But wasn't that weird, though? The cop questioning you like that."

"Yes, it was. I knew without a doubt in my mind that this man was about to lock my ass up. And especially after he flashed his flashlight at me. I was a freaking basket case. But thank God, I got out of that."

"Yes, thank God. Because I don't know what I would've done if that cop had locked you up."

"And neither would I." I agreed.

Nick and I talked for another ten minutes. It took us that long to drink the rest of our beverage and eat our pastry. He tried to get me to give him another round of sex but I told him that he had to wait. "The quicker you go there and come back, the quicker you'll be able to get some of this wet-wet!" I enticed him.

He smiled and stood up on his feet. "Say no more." He said and then he raced to the bathroom and hopped in the shower. He was in the shower and out in less than five minutes. When he came out of the bathroom, he called his cousin and told him to come and pick him up. Surprisingly, Raymond was already in the area and told Nick that he'd be outside of the hotel room in less than two minutes.

On Nick's way out, he gave me a passionate kiss. And then he slapped me on the butt. "The keys to my truck are on the table just in case you need to run out. Oh yeah, and be ready when I get back." He instructed me.

"Don't worry. I will." I assured him and then I closed the door and locked it.

Immediately after he and Raymond drove out of the parking lot of the hotel, I climbed back on the bed and turned the channel of the TV to one of the movie channels programmed in the cable box. I began to watch the movie Zombie Land. It was somewhat of a corny zombie movie, but it was the only thing running, so I had no other choice but to watch it. I watched the entire movie, plus the movie after that. Before I knew it, I had watched a total of four hours of movies. I even realized that Nick hadn't come back to the hotel yet, either.

I didn't have Raymond's cell phone number, so I wasn't able to call him. And instead of sulking about it, I ordered a pizza from a local pizza place and had it delivered. When the black guy delivered my pizza, I paid him and then I closed the door and locked it. My stomach had been growling for the last two hours so it didn't take me long to devour the first two slices. I tried to eat a third slice but I couldn't eat it all, so I put it back in the box and lied down across the bed.

I tried to watch a few shows on TV but I couldn't concentrate. I couldn't get Nick off my mind. It's been close to five hours since he's been gone and that worries me. Thinking of the endless possibilities that could be wrong wasn't sitting well with me. "Nick, where are you?" I mumbled. And then out the blue, I heard the keycard activation magnet click on the other side of the door and then the door opened. My face lit up when I saw Nick walk into the room. I leaped up from the bed and embraced him. "Where have you been? I was worried about you." I told him.

"I'm sorry about that. My fucking cousin had me running around on a goose chase and I ended up with nothing."

"What happened?" I asked him after he took a seat on the edge of the bed and I sat next to him.

"He told me that he applied for a loan from his bank and they approved them for the twenty-grand. So, all he had to do was go to the bank and pick up the check. Well, when we got to the bank, I stayed in the car. I waited in his car for almost a fucking hour. So, when he finally came back to the car empty-handed, you know I was about to take that dude's head off."

"What did he say?"

"He gave me some bogus ass excuse talking about the bank said he needed to provide them with proof of his wife's income and proof of collateral before they can finalize the loan. But there's a catch."

"What is it?"

"He doesn't want his wife to know that I lent him the money to get their house. He wants her to believe that he was saving up the money and that's how they got it."

"So, what are you going to do?"

"I told him that I'm giving him until tomorrow to come up with my money and that if he doesn't, then I'm burning his fucking house down. I'll definitely be able to get it then, especially after he put in the insurance claim for it."

"Think he's gonna come up with it?"

"I don't know what he's gonna do. But better come up with something or suffer the consequences." Nick said with finality and I believed him.

$$\longleftrightarrow$$

Nick was pretty pissed off by the fact that he wasn't successful at getting his money back from Raymond. After talking with him for a while and then giving him more of this hot and wet sex I had for him, he became relaxed and intoxicating. I think we burst like three to four orgasms. It felt like magic, having him inside of me. And I will do everything in my power to keep things just like this.

TIMES UP

I woke up to the noise of the shower water running in the bathroom and when I looked at the time on the alarm clock and noticed that it was 8:47, I knew Nick was getting ready so he could run out and get his money from his cousin Raymond. When he came out of the bathroom, he got dress, drowned me with a ton of kisses and then he got ready to leave. "How long will you be this time?" I wondered aloud.

"Not long. I'll call you when I'm on my way back." He replied as he walked towards the door.

"Give me the phone number to the burner phone you got on you so I can call you if I need something," I said.

Nick stopped, turned around and then he grabbed the pen and pad he saw on the table. "I'm writing the number on this paper just in case." He told me.

"All right. Be careful out there."

He smiled at me. "Don't worry, I will." He replied and started walking back towards the door.

"Hey wait," I said and jumped up from the bed. "Give me a kiss." I insisted.

After we locked lips and kissed a couple of times, he slapped me on my butt and told me to be ready when he comes back because we will jump on the road and head out west as soon as he gets back.

I assured him that I would be ready when he got back. After we kissed for the last and final time, I watched him get into his truck and headed out of the hotel parking lot.

My heart started fluttering again as I thought about how lucky I was to have a man like Nick in my life. I know it's hard to understand how quickly I fell in love with Nick but as I see it, my love for him was already planted inside of me. When I saw him interacting with other women I would feel a sense of jealousy inside. I even envied women that he'd bring on double dates with Dylan and I. I thought what I was feeling for him was a crush. But, as I see it now, I know that I was falling in love with him. I can't say how long I'm going to be under his spell, so I hope it's forever.

$\longleftrightarrow$

While Nick was out taking care of his business with Raymond, I hopped in the shower and bathe so I could be ready when Nick came back. The words and melody of New Edition's new song, Just for Me & You, rang in my head and all I could think about was embarking on a new journey with Nick. I know that this will sound selfish and maybe inconceivable, but having Nick with me every step of the way has allowed me to move on with my life without Dylan. Nick has become a healthy distraction and I owe him my life for that. I thought my life was going to be filled with constant pain and depression but it hasn't. Love came in and landed at the right location and at the right time. What more could I ask for?

I slipped on a sweatshirt and a pair of sweatpants that belonged to Nick since I hadn't had a chance to go out and buy some new clothes. I figured when Nick and I get on the road and head out to LA, then I'd be able to buy myself a few nice pairs of jeans and shirts to match. Planning in my head where Nick and I are going to stop to shop while we're on the road, I heard a knock on the door. I immediately looked at the clock and noticed that it was 11:10. My heart rate picked up speed as I build up the nerve to stand up on my feet. "Who the fuck could that be?" I whispered as I tiptoed towards the door.

I was hoping that it was Nick knocking because he forgot to grab the magnetic keycard, but when I looked back at the TV stand and realized that he'd taken it with him, my heart sped up even faster. I was literally about to have an anxiety attack. With each step I took, the more afraid I become. Boom! Boom! Boom! The knocks seemed to get louder the closer I got to the door. "Is anyone in there? It's housekeeping." I heard a lady yell from the other side of the door. After hearing a woman's voice identify herself as a housekeeper, I felt completely relieved. And since I was closer to the window than the door, I grabbed the curtain and pulled it back just enough so I could see what she wanted. But as soon as I peered outside, I noticed that it was a woman from housekeeping, but I couldn't see her face because she had completely turned around. Her back was facing the door and she was facing in the opposite direction. Someone else had her attention so when I looked in that direction, my heart dropped into the pit of my stomach when I realized that she was making hand gestures to two plainclothes cops that were parked in an unmarked car. I couldn't fucking believe it. The cops had one of the housekeepers knock on the door to try and lure me to the door. But my question is, who are they? The name of the room isn't in my name nor Nick's so are they looking for us? And if they are, then who are they? FBI? U.S. Marshalls? Or local cops? The thought of not knowing who they are is extremely terrifying. I just hoped that they're not there when

Nick returns. Because if they are in fact looking for us, then we are screwed.

I backed away from the window and stood a few feet away from it so I could get a good look at the front of the door and the entire parking. Petrified that Nick may come back while the cops are still here, I grabbed one of his burner cell phones from his suitcase, activated it and then I keyed in the cell phone number that he wrote down on the pad of paper. I took a seat on the edge of the bed after it started ringing and waited for him to answer it. Thankfully, he answered it on the second ring. "Hello," He said.

I got up from the bed and went into the bathroom to make sure no one on the outside of these walls could hear me talk. "Hello," He said again.

I hurried up and closed the bathroom door quietly and then I said, "Where are you?"

"I'm with Raymond. I'm sitting in his car while he's inside of the bank. Why is everything all right?"

"There's a couple of cops in plains clothes sitting outside in their car watching our room."

"How you know that?"

"Because they had a housekeeper knock on the door to see if I'll open it. And when I didn't, she started using hand motions to let the cops know that no one was inside. Nick, I'm really scared."

"Just calm down. You're gonna be all right."

"What if the housekeeper uses her key to open the door?"

"If they were going to do that, they would've gotten her to do it the first time. They don't have a search warrant. So, if you would've opened the door and saw you, then they would've had probable cause to come inside the room."

"Are you sure?"

"Of course, I'm sure. So, take a deep breath and everything will work out how it's supposed to."

"But what if it doesn't? What if they do get a search warrant and come in here and arrest me while you're gone?"

"That's not gonna happen."

"Did you get Raymond to pay the front desk for another night? Cause' if he didn't then I'm gonna have to leave out of this room and there's gonna be nowhere for me to hide. I'm gonna be out in the opening."

"Kira, the room has already been paid for. So, I need you to snap out of it because you're not making this easy for me. I told you that you're gonna be fine. Just sit tight and don't answer the door, okay."

"Okay," I said.

"All right, now check it out, Raymond got me somewhere over here in the French Quarters, sitting outside a bank. He said that he's gonna give me five grand after he comes out of there and then he's going to take me to some guys that he owes him a couple of grand, so I'll be back at the hotel as soon as I can."

"Doesn't sound like he's gonna give you back all of your money."

"Oh yes, he is. I just screamed on his ass and told him that if he didn't give me all my money back that I was going to pistol whip his ass and burn down his house."

"Did you really say that?"

"Yeah, I did. He talked to me in a disrespectful manner when Hailey opened the door this morning and let me in their house."

"What did he say?"

"He asked me why was I there? He said that I shouldn't be there because he didn't call me and give me permission to be there."

"Are you serious?"

"You fucking right I'm serious. I damn near cursed that dude out. I told him that I had a lot of shit going on in my life that he didn't want to get on my bad side. So, he finally got a grip on himself and apologized to me after Hailey went into their bedroom."

"Nick, please be careful."

"I will. Now, stay away from the door and the window and I'll be there as soon as I can."

"Call me when you're on your way."

"I will."

"I love you," I told him. I said it with conviction.

"I love you too Kira." He replied and then we ended the call.

THIS SITUATION JUST GOT STICKY

I know Nick told me to stay away from the window but I couldn't help myself. I needed to keep my eyes on my surroundings. After watching the cops stake out my hotel room for a little over 30 minutes, they finally gave up and left. Boy, was I relieved to see them leave. But for the life of me, I couldn't figure out who they could've been.

The car they were in had Louisiana license plates, so who the hell were those guys? Were they Feds? Local cops? What? I swear, not knowing who those guys were had me on edge. And if Nick doesn't hurry up and get back here then I may have a nervous breakdown. God, please look after me.

One hour passed. Then two hours passed. And then the third hour kept by, I picked up the burner phone and tried to get Nick back on the phone but I couldn't. His cell phone kept going straight to voicemail. I couldn't leave him any messages because of the type of phones he and I had. Burner cell phones are only for incoming and outgoing calls. Leaving messages is a no-no, especially if you're trying to stay under the radar. And in our case, that's exactly what we were doing. I even thought about getting Raymond on the phone, but I didn't know his cell phone number. I didn't even have his wife's Hailey number either. I was like a man lost at sea. "Ugh! Who else can I call?" I said aloud, but so only I could hear me.

When hour five and six came and gone, I was still sitting in the hotel room alone and worried. I paced the hotel room floor back and forth at least five dozen times. I couldn't stay still for nothing in the world. "Nick baby, where are you? And why aren't you answering your phone?" I mumbled to myself, as anxiety mounted inside of me. My stomach had knots tossing and turning inside of me too. "Baby, where are you? Please get back here safe and sound?" I continued to mumble to myself.

After the seventh hour and Nick hadn't returned to the hotel nor answered his cell phone, I got fed up with waiting for him and decided to take a chance at sliding out of this room undetected and flagging a cab. With the day turning into night, I figured that I'll be fine outside just as long as I don't bring any attention to myself. Keep my head down and my ears open.

I sat by the window and peered out of it for five minutes until I realized that there were no strange cars in or around the parking lot. The housekeepers had clocked off for the rest of the day too so I knew that right now was the perfect time to make my way out of the room. And that's exactly what I did.

Like a flash of lighting, I grabbed my handbag and the magnetic key card and made a dash for it. I was out of my hotel room on 300 ft. away from the hotel in a matter of one-and-a-half-minute flat.

It only took me another minute to flag down a cab too. "Look, sir, I don't know the name of the street I'm going to. But I do know how to get there." I said to a black older gentleman.

"Do you know how far it is from where we are now?" He wanted to know.

"About a five to six-minute drive." I guessed.

"I'll tell you what, give me twenty bucks now and when we get to your destination, you can pay me the rest." He bargained with me, I figured that he thought that I might run out on paying him, so I didn't give him a hard time. I paid him the $20 he asked for and then we were on our way.

My heart rate picked up again as the cab driver drove in the direction of Raymond and Hailey's house.

It only took a matter of 10 minutes to arrive at the house. When we pulled up Nick's truck was nowhere in sight, but Raymond and Hailey's car was parked out front. "You can let me off right here," I told the cab driver. After I paid him, I slid out of the back seat and headed towards the front door.

I only had to knock on the door once to get Raymond to open it and let me in. "Hey Raymond, I'm looking for Nick. Is he here?" I asked him even though I knew that there was a possibility that he wasn't being that his truck wasn't outside.

"No. He left hours ago."

"What time? Because he didn't come back to the hotel."

"I don't know. Maybe like four hours ago." Raymond replied. But for some reason, he wasn't convincing. He was acting like he was hiding something from me.

"Can I come in?" I asked him after looking over my shoulders. I had to make sure that those cops I saw earlier today, wasn't lurking from around the corner of one of these houses on this block.

"Sure. Come in." He replied.

I walked into the house and saw Hailey sitting on the sofa. She acted like she was fully engrossed in a movie that was on TV. I said hello to her and then I turned my focus back on Raymond. "Did he say where he was going?" I asked him.

"No, he didn't. So, I assumed that he was going back to the hotel."

"Raymond, I'm worried because this isn't like Nick. We made plans to leave the hotel and head out." I said.

"He's probably there now looking for you."

"If he was, then he would've called me by now," I said confidently. But the reaction I got back from Raymond, told me that something was wrong. "Raymond, please tell me where Nick is. I know you know." I pressured him.

"We don't know. He left here hours ago."

I looked at Hailey and then I looked back at Raymond. "He's with Cali isn't he?" I got up the gumption to ask.

"No, he's not with her."

"Then where is he?" I became irritated.

"I don't know." Raymond wouldn't let up.

I turned my attention to Hailey. "Hailey, I promise I won't get mad if you guys tell me that Nick is with Cali. I just need to know that he's all right."

Before Hailey could utter one word, someone knocked on the front door. Everyone, including myself, turned their attention towards the door. My heart started racing because I didn't know whether to stand there and see who was on the other side of the door or run because it could be the cops looking for Nick and I. Either way, I was going to get my answer.

Raymond walked towards the front door and said, "Who is it?"

"It's me, Cali." I heard her say. Now I all I needed to do was see who she was with.

MONEY OVER FAMILY

Raymond opens the front door and Cali comes inside the house looking shocked as ever because she sees me in the house. After she looks at me from head to toe, she looks at Hailey who is sitting on the sofa with a facial expression of worry. Raymond didn't help things because he looked worried too. "What's going on?" She asked them. And before either one of them answered her question, she looked at me from head to toe. "Did I come at the wrong time?" she wondered aloud as she placed her purse down on the coffee table in front of Hailey.

"Everything is fine. Kira is here because Nick left here and never went back to the hotel where Kira was." Raymond spoke first.

"Was he with you?" I didn't hesitate to ask her.

"No, I haven't seen him since he left from here yesterday," Cali answered me. "Whatcha' think he ran off and left you here to fin for yourself?" She continued and then she chuckled.

"Sorry to burst your bubble. But Nick would never leave me." I assured her. And then I looked around the room and searched everyone's face for a sign of guilt. Immediately after I scanned Hailey's face, I saw her holding something black in her hands. She was trying her best to keep whatever she had in her hands, completely covered.

"Then where is he?" Cali probed me with a little smirk on her face. She appeared to be enjoying the fact that I was there looking for Nick.

"We don't know where he is. He left here hours ago." Raymond answered.

"When she got here and didn't see him, she automatically thought that he was with you." Hailey chimed in.

Cali smiled in a more grimace like expression and walked towards me. "I'm sorry to say that he isn't with me. But I'm sure that he's gonna call me later after he tucks you in bed." She commented in a spiteful manner. It felt like she was trying to get a reaction out of me. And after I stood there for a moment and realized that she was wearing my patience thins I gave her exactly what she wanted.

Before she got within arms reach of me, I turned my body slightly towards the left and eased by her.

And in a two to three-second count, I snatched her purse up from the coffee table, and grabbed her pistol from it and pointed directly at her. "Bitch, I'm gonna ask you nicely to get the fuck back!" I spat. Game time was over. I wasn't in the mood to play mind games with any of these dumb assholes.

"What are you doing? Give me my gun back!" Cali snapped and started walking slowly towards me.

"You better get back before I lay your ass out in here!" I warned her.

Cali chuckled. "Do you even know how to use that?" He asked me as she stood a few feet away from me.

"Move another step bitch, and I will show you." I threatened.

As soon as Cali stopped in her tracks, I looked back at Hailey and asked her to opened her hands. Shocked by my questions, she sat there looking dumbfounded. "Show me what you have in your hands," I demanded.

"Why are you asking her what she's got in her hand?" Raymond asked. I could tell that he was nervous for her.

"I don't have anything in my hands." She finally said.

I took two steps towards her and demanded that she open her hands. And when she didn't do it, I pointed Cali's gun at her and said, "Bitch, if you don't show me what you have in your hands, I'm gonna splatter your brains all over that sofa."

"When you came here with Nick, we welcomed you in our home with open arms." Raymond tried to say, but I told him to shut up.

Through my peripheral vision I saw Cali leap towards me, and without much thought, I slightly turned in her direction, aimed the gun at her and shot it twice. Pop! Pop! And like a predator dominating their prey, Cali collapsed down on the floor. Hailey screamed at the top of her voice. "Auuuuuuuuuwww! What have you done? You killed my friend." Hailey cried out.

I turned back towards Hailey and pointed the gun at her. "Shut the fuck up and open your fucking hands!" I roared. Without any more hesitation, Hailey finally opened her hands and revealed what she was trying to hide. "That's Nick's burner phone. Where is he?" I demanded to know.

Sobbing uncontrollably, Hailey dropped Nick's cell phone down on the floor and buried her face in the palm of her hands. Raymond started crying himself and that's when I told him to shut the fuck up and take a seat next to Hailey on the sofa. After he done it, I pointed Cali's gun at Hailey and threatened to kill her next if he doesn't tell me where Nick was.

"He's dead." Hailey bellowed after she lifted up her head from the palm of her hands.

Taken aback by her answer, my heart collapsed into the pit of my stomach. "He's what?" I asked her. I needed for her to repeat herself.

"He's dead." She cried out.

After hearing the words that Nick was dead, I wasn't willing to accept that. They had to be wrong. I had just spoken to him hours ago, so they had to be wrong. I mean, I'll accept the fact that he ran off with another woman or that he got jammed up with the cops that were staking out our hotel room. But being dead, was the last thing I wanted to hear.

"Raymond where is Nick?" I roared, pointing the gun directly at him.

"I didn't mean to shoot him. We started arguing about the money I owed him and the next thing I know he pulled out his gun and aimed it at me. I tried to take the gun from him and it went off. I swear, I didn't mean for it to happen." He continued to sob. But I wasn't fazed by his tears. The sight of him was making me sick to my stomach. In my eyes, he was a weak ass man. All he had to do was give Nick back his money. That's it.

Feelings of hurt and sorrow began to consume me because I've just lost another man that I loved. What am I going to do now? "Where is he?" I asked him.

"He's in our back bathroom," Raymond replied as the tears continued to fall from his eyes.

"Please don't kill us." Hailey began to beg.

"Yes, please don't kill us." Raymond chimed in.

"Both of y'all shut the fuck up and stand up on your feet!" I spat. One by one they got up and stood up. "Take me to the back bathroom," I instructed them both.

Hailey walked in the direction of their bedroom first with Raymond in tow. I followed them closely just in case they wanted to do something stupid. "I'm telling y'all right now, not to do something really stupid."

"We won't. We will do anything you tell us to." Raymond insisted.

"I said to shut the fuck up!" I snapped and jammed the barrel of Cali's gun in his back. He flinched a little and skipped a step as he walked behind Hailey. Immediately after they entered their bedroom, they continued on towards the bathroom. "Open the door." I continued instructing them.

"I can't do it." Hailey cried as she stepped to the side of the bathroom door.

I nudged Raymond in the back with the gun once more. "Open the door," I demanded.

Raymond took three steps towards the bathroom door and then he opened it. There in plain view, I saw

Nick lying in his own pool of blood. I also saw two gunshot wounds to his chest. His lifeless body was beginning to be unbearable to look at so I turned my attention back towards Hailey and Raymond and aimed the gun at them. "You took the only man left in the world away from me and now you're gonna pay for it." I started off saying, as the tears started rolling down my face.

"It was an accident." Raymond blurted out. But it was too late, I had already pulled the trigger. Pop! Pop! I shot Raymond first and then I turned the gun on Hailey and shot her next. Pop! Pop! Both Raymond and Hailey's lifeless bodies collapsed onto the floor in their bedroom. Blood from their bodies spewed out onto the carpet surrounding them. But I could care less. They took Nick from me and now I've got to go on with my life without him.

"I am so sorry baby." I started sobbing, while I looked at him. I wanted to get down on the floor and hold him in my arms but I knew that I couldn't leave any of my DNA near him.

"I will never forget you." I managed to say through my cries and then I blew a kiss at him. "Come on girl, you gotta get out of here before somebody comes here and sees you," I said to myself, as a way to snap out of my feelings and use my head.

I sprinted out of Raymond and Hailey's bedroom and headed back into the living room where Cali's body was. I snatched Cali's purse up from the table and looked inside of it. After seeing that her car keys were inside, I grabbed Nick's burner cell phone from the floor where Hailey obviously dropped it and then I grabbed Cali's Rolex watch and Cartier bracelets from her wrist. I mean, it's not like she's going to be able to wear them anymore. I'm gonna put them to good use.

With everything I need in hand, I made my way towards the front door. I was out of the house and into Cali's black, Range Rover sport in less than one minute. Thankfully, it was night outside, so I knew that no one would ever be able to identify me even if they did say they saw a black woman getting into this truck. I was home free, even if I was on the run. I can't say what's going to happen after I leave this place. But I will be able to say that I survived another *Sticky Situation*.

SNEAK PEEK AT
"GREEN EYED BANDIT"
(IN STORES NOW)

PROLOGUE

My heart wouldn't accept what was going on around me. But my eyes knew better. Watching these monsters torture my sister Shelby had become unbearable. And every time I tried to look away, one of those goons snatched my head back by yanking my hair. "Nah bitch, you're gonna watch this." The guy roared and then he spit in my face.

My sister Shelby and I had always played a game or two of Russian roulette with our lives, but as fate would have it, our time had ran out. There was no way we were going to walk out of here alive. Even Shelby's probation officer Ms. Welch wasn't going to leave out of here breathing. Unfortunately, for her she planned an after hours home visit to our apartment so she could check on Shelby, and walked into a death trap. I knew she wished she had kept her field visits during business hours because now she's gotten herself into a bloody mess.

There were three guys surrounding us. They kicked in our front door and bum-rushed our apartment with their guns drawn and ready to fire. I knew why they were here so I tried to escape out of the apartment from our second story bathroom window, but Rocko quickly apprehended me and started the beating.

All three men looked menacing. They were average in height but they made up for their height in weight. They had to be at least two hundred pounds easy because the first time Shelby and I got hit in the face, it sounded like our jawbones cracked. Shelby screamed from the minute Rocko snatched her up by her neck until the time he hit her in her face. I saw the horror in her eyes and I saw our lives flash right before my eyes. It was going to be a sad night for the both of us. God help us all.

Breon and his henchmen came equipped with rope and duct tape and tied us up to our kitchen chairs so we wouldn't have another chance to run. They even tied gags around our mouths to prevent us from letting the outside world know what was going on inside of our apartment. And it worked, because halfway into the beating, Ms. Welch knocked on the front door. "Open the door, Ms. Martin, it's me, Ms. Welch." We all heard her say.

All three men looked at one another and then they looked at Shelby and I. The guy Breon wanted to know who was at the door. He pulled the duct tape from Shelby's mouth good enough for her to answer his questions. "It's my P.O. and she isn't going to leave until somebody opens the door," she warned him.

Breon motioned one of the guys to look through the peephole to see what Shelby's probation officer was doing on the other side of the door. The guy tiptoed to the front door and when he stepped on the loose wooden board directly in front of the door, it cracked and Ms. Welch heard it loud and clear. "Shelby, I hear you in there. Now if you don't open this door right now, I am going to have the police come and do it for me," she threatened, but no one moved. Breon waited for a moment to think and then a couple seconds later he instructed the guy at the door to open the door. "What if she wants to come in?" he objected.

"Just shut up and open it," Breon demanded in a low like whisper. But his pitch wasn't low enough because Ms. Welch heard him. "I hear you all talking in there. Now this will be the last time I tell you to open this door before I call the police for their assistance," she warned us.

The guy at the front door looked back at Breon once more. "Do it now," Breon instructed him once again. I could see that Breon was getting a little aggravated. The guy saw it too and decided to do as he was told. He turned back towards the front door and pulled the mask from his head. And not even a second later, he unlocked and opened the front door. The way our chairs were placed around the kitchen table, Shelby couldn't see the front door but I could.

Ms. Welch stood there before him and went into question mode that instant. "Where is Shelby?" she asked him.

"She's not here," the guy lied.

Ms. Welch sensed that he lied too, that's why she tried to look around him to get a good look into the apartment. The guy was too quick for her and moved to block her view. She didn't like that one bit. "Are you trying to hide something from me?" she questioned him once more.

"No, I'm not."

"What is your name young man?" her questions continued.

"My name is Antonio." He said flatly.

"Well Mr. Antonio, my name is Ms. Welch and I am Shelby's probation officer. And I am here today because she lied to me about sending in copies of her check stubs. Now, I'm going to need you to step aside so I can enter into this apartment."

"But I told you she's not here."

"I remember you saying that, but as her probation officer, I have the right to search her dwelling at which time I see fit. And today would be one of those times," she tried to say it as politely as she could. Ms. Welch was one evil ass lady and when it came to home visits, she meant business. And the fact that this guy wasn't going to allow her to do what she wanted, she wasn't too happy about that.

While all of the commotions went down at the front door, Breon realized that his sidekick wasn't handling the situation with Shelby's probation officer as swiftly as he'd liked, so he stormed to the front door with his gun behind his back to see if he could make her go away. But what Breon failed to do was cover Shelby's mouth up before he walked off and left us in the kitchen. And as soon as Breon turned the corner, Shelby screamed as loud as she could and said, "Ms. Welch run and call the police."

Breon turned back around and rushed towards Shelby. When he got within arms reach of her, he lunged back and punched her in the face as hard as he could. The force behind his punch knocked Shelby backwards onto the floor. And when I thought I'd seen enough, he started kicking her in her side while her arms were tied behind her back and her ankles tied to the legs of the chair. She looked so helpless on the floor and I couldn't do a thing to help her. She cried her poor heart out while Breon kicked and stomped her with his fucking Timberland boots. I swear if I had the strength to break loose from these restraints, I'd have his fucking head on a chopping block, digging his eyes out of his fucking head.

While Breon was beating the shit out of my sister, the other guy had no choice but to grab Ms. Welch and drag her into the apartment. She put up a big fight to get away from him but when Breon's other henchman saw that his partner needed help in getting Ms. Welch under control, he went to his aid. With both men attacking her at the same time, Ms. Welch didn't have a fighting chance. And after she suffered consistent blows to her body and head, she lost consciousness.

"Breon, we gon' need some help picking her big ass up from the floor. I heard one guy say.

"One of y'all help me pick this bitch up from the floor first," Breon demanded. He had stopped hitting and kicking Shelby by this time. So, after Breon and one of the other guys helped sit Shelby's chair back on its feet, all three of them managed to pick Ms. Welch up and sat her in a chair next to us. They didn't waste any time bounding and gagging her.

I could tell that she was clinging to life. And right before the beating started, she begged those fucking monsters to spare her. "I'm not the one you want." She pleaded. But they ignored her cries and proceeded to beat her across her face. I literally cried for her and Shelby, because I felt their pain and I knew that my time was coming next.

Breon's heartless ass washed Shelby's blood from his arms and hands. He dried them off by wiping his palms directly across the thigh part of his jeans. I watched him very closely through my glassy eyes. I was furious about everything I had witnessed and I wanted my revenge. But that feat looked impossible from where I was sitting, so I sat quickly and prayed a silent prayer.

"Don't close those green eyes now bitch! 'Cause your ass is next." Breon warned me and then I heard his footsteps coming in my direction. I stopped midway in my prayer and opened my eyes. I tried to scream when I saw that he had his gun pointed directly at Shelby, but I was unable to do so with the duct tape wrapped tightly around my mouth. Tears started falling rapidly. And my heart began to beat erratically. She was done and I knew it. So, I took one last look at her and watched Breon pull the trigger. BOOM!

CHAPTER ONE
THE COME UP

The temperature throughout the hotel suite was set at 70 degrees, but sweat pellets emerged from the pores of my forehead and underneath my armpits like I was sitting inside of a fucking sauna. I swear I couldn't get out of this place quick enough. I had just taken a bunch of cash from a black, Marc Jacobs handcrafted leather wallet that belonged to this guy my sister Shelby was fucking in the next room. When I first arrived in the hotel room, I heard Shelby moaning like her mind was going bad. It sounded like she was getting her pussy ate and when I peeped in on the action, my suspicions were confirmed. That cracker she had feasting between her legs was putting in overtime. I almost got up the nerve to ask him to give me some of his tongue action. But after I snapped back into reality about what I came here to do, I decided against it.

171

A few minutes after I started going through the man's things, I realized he and Shelby had switched positions. "Damn girl, you sure know how to suck the meat off my dick!" I heard him say to Shelby.

"I make you……..feel……..good, huh?" Shelby replied between licks.

I laughed of course because Shelby was a class act. She was a master at making guys weak at their knees. Shelby was a sexy, 135lbs., bombshell. She was a very pretty young woman with a body to die for. Her caramel complexion, long, straight, dark brown hair, and her big hazel colored eyes were the perfect combination. It wasn't hard to tell that she was half Cuban and black. From the time we were young girls, boys would always throw themselves at her. And while she had them literally eating out of her hands, she could never keep a man around long enough to have a solid relationship, so she did the next best thing; trick with them. She gave them what they wanted and in return, they gave her what she wanted. It was a win-win situation in her eyes.

The joker she had in her grasp tonight was a white investment banker from Maryland in town for a conference. According to the driver's license in his wallet, his name was Alex Leman. He was born in 1962, he resided in the city of Baltimore, and he was an organ donor. How freaking patriotic of him? The old dude had a soft spot for humanity. Sorry to say he had a kinky side to him as well. And since tonight was his last night in town, Shelby and I seized this opportunity to come up on some major dough. I got him for every crisp one hundred dollar bill he had tucked away in his wallet. I hadn't had a chance to count them, but there had to be at least twelve of them in all. He also had a few major credit cards like an American Express and Discover card, but I left them alone. I wasn't about to get caught on camera in some department store trying to buy a bunch of bullshit with stolen credit cards. I wanted my money free and clear. Too bad, I can't say the same about Shelby. She'd snatch this guy's credit cards up in a heartbeat. It didn't matter to her that she was on probation because she had already been charged and convicted of credit card fraud a year ago. But I cared and as long as she turned the tricks and I did the taking, I vowed to do things my way.

Immediately after I had taken all of the money this guy Alex had, I stuffed it inside of my pants pocket and headed towards the door of the hotel suite. But before I could sneak back out of the hotel room, some asshole knocked on the fucking door. I panicked and almost pissed in my pants. How in the hell could someone come at a time like this? I rushed to the door and looked through the peephole. To my surprise, my co-worker Mitch from room service was standing on the other side of the door with a bottle of champagne in a bucket of ice and two champagne glasses placed on a rolling table. My first reaction was to open the door and tell Mitch to carry his ass, but then I realized how he'd react seeing me in this room, so I decided against it. Two seconds later, Mitch knocked on the door again and then he yelled out the words, "Room service."

I literally almost passed out right there in the hallway. But when I heard Alex scramble to his feet to get the door, I jumped into the hallway closet and slid the door closed. "I'm coming," I heard Shelby's sex partner yell as soon as he got within several feet of the door to his suite.

I couldn't see Alex as he made his way to the door, but I heard every move he made from the time he opened the door to let Mitch roll the table inside the room until he started questioning Shelby, who had followed him to the door. "Wait a minute," he said and then he fell silent.

"What's the matter?" Shelby questioned him.

"I had over fifteen hundred dollars in my fucking wallet and now it's gone." he said.

"Are you sure?" Shelby asked.

"You goddamn right I'm sure!" he roared.

"Why are you snapping at me?" I heard Shelby say.

"Because my money is gone and you've been the only one in this room."

"So, you're accusing me of taking your fucking money? she snapped back.

"Who else could've taken it?" Alex stood his ground.

"First of all, I've been by your side the entire time I've been in this fucking room. So, how in the hell could I have taken the money?" Shelby reasoned.

Before Alex responded to Shelby, Mitch interjected, "Sir, don't worry about it. Just call room service and have them charge the champagne and the strawberries to your room." Then I heard the door close.

Seconds later, I heard Shelby say, "I can't believe you just accused me of stealing your fucking money."

But Alex didn't respond to her. He remained completely quiet. They continued to stand outside of the closet door, so I was literally in the center of all the action. I just wished that I could see what they were doing.

"Why the fuck are you just standing there and looking at me like you're insane?" Shelby continued.

So again, I waited to hear Alex's response. And to my surprise, he didn't utter one word. I did, however, hear sudden movement and then I heard a loud boom sound. "What the fuck are you doing? Get off of me." Shelby said, her voice was barely audible.

"I going to kill you, you black bitch!" he grinded his teeth. "You're gonna wish you never laid eyes on me." He continued.

Then I heard Shelby coughing. "Get off me!" She managed to say.

My heart raced as I listened to the commotion outside the closet door. It was apparent that Alex was choking Shelby to her death. And that's when it popped in my head that if I didn't stop him, I'd have one dead sister. So, within seconds, I burst out of the closet door and was able to witness first hand how badly Alex was hurting her.

Right after I burst onto the scene, I noticed how shocked they both were to see me. "Get the fuck off of her!" I demanded as I stormed towards his 5'10 frame. He looked like he weighed 150lbs., but that didn't at all intimidate me, even though I was at least 30lbs., lighter. I used to run track back when I was in high school, so I was physically fit.

"What the fuck?" Alex uttered from his lips. He was definitely at a lost for words when he realized that he and Shelby weren't alone. And while he had Shelby's back against the wall, he had both of his hands around her neck, leaving himself vulnerable for me to intervene. This guy was on a mission to choke the life out of her. So I lunged towards the back of his head with my fist and clocked him as hard as I could. I followed that blow with several more punches, and then I threw my right arm around his neck and grabbed him into a chokehold. "Let her go," I demanded as I applied pressure to his neck.

He struggled to keep Shelby within his grasp and when he realized that I wasn't going to let him go, he started loosening the grip around her neck and then he finally let her go. "Alright. I let her go. Now you let me go," he pleaded.

"If I let you go, you ain't gonna try no funny shit, right?" I questioned him.

"No. I swear I won't," he assured me. But I wasn't feeling his answer. Something told me that this guy couldn't be trusted. He had already tried to murk Shelby, so why wouldn't he try to throw shade on both of us in this damn hotel room? If he really wanted to fuck us over, he could call the cops on our asses and get me and Shelby locked up for trespassing and robbery and that would not have been a good look on our part.

"How do I know if you'll try some dumb shit?" I asked him.

"Look, lady, I don't want any problems. Just take your friend and leave and I'll forget that any of this happened." He managed to say while I continued to hold him in the chokehold.

I looked at Shelby who was only three feet away from me. I searched her face for any sign about which course of action we should take. And when she instructed me to keep him hemmed up until she gathered up her things, I did just that. "A'ight. But hurry up." I yelled aloud as she disappeared into the other room.

Meanwhile, Alex became a little antsy while I had him in the chokehold. "You do know that I could have both of you bitches arrested" he commented.

I tightened the grip around his neck just a bit more. "Shut the hell up before I call your wife and tell her how you like eating black pussy," I said.

After I threatened to spill the beans on his ass, he immediately changed his tune. "Look, just get out of my hotel room and take your friend with you," he said.

Moments later, Shelby showed back up fully dressed with her handbag clutched tightly in her right hand. "Come on, let's go," she said. And then she rushed towards the door. ....,

Once, Shelby, had the door opened, I released my grip from the white guy's neck and raced out of the door behind her. She and I ran into the hallway and bumped into Mitch. Mitch was a middle-aged, metrosexual white guy with feminine behavior and everything to prove. He stood there with mere shock written all over his face. But I was even more shocked than anything. I thought he'd carried his ass back to the kitchen, but I was so wrong. And now that Shelby and I were caught red-handed, I needed to come up with something really quick. Mitch was one of the hotel's ass kissers. He'd blow the whistle on anyone if it meant he'd get a promotion. So, I knew whatever I said to him had to be convincing or else. "Mitch, what's going on?" I asked trying to prevent myself from panting. I had just run out of a man's hotel room after holding him against his will, so I was very tired.

"Well, I was on my way back to room 521 to make sure everything was okay with our guest and his female companion." Mitch began to say and then he turned his attention towards Shelby. "And from the looks of it, I can see that she's fine."

I knew Mitch was being a smart ass. And I played along. "Yeah, she's fine. Luckily, I was still at work when she called me to come and talk some sense into that guy. And thank God he managed to find his money just as we were about to leave." I lied.

"Lucky her," he replied sarcastically.

"Well, I appreciate the fact that you thought about her enough to come all the way back up here to check on her. That's noble of you." I replied with a fake smile.

"I was actually more concerned about Mr. Leman," he pointed out.

"Well, it doesn't matter. Either way, your intentions were good, so keep up the good work." I told him and then I gave him a pat on the shoulder and made my way to the stairwell. Shelby followed down behind me like she was my shadow. I figured it was best to leave the hotel by taking the stairs just in case that white cat Alex had a change of heart and wanted to call security on our asses. Besides that, I didn't want to run into another one of my co-workers. Seeing Mitch was enough for one night.

Thankfully, Shelby and I made it out the hotel without running into another one of my co-workers, plus we were fifteen hundred dollars richer. On our way up Atlantic Avenue, she and I both laughed at how stupid that white guy looked after he realized that his money had been taken. I even elaborated about how he looked when he saw me jump out of the closet. "Did you see the look on his face after he realized I was in the room with y'all?" I said.

"Yeah, I saw it. But check it out; I was even more shocked to see you myself. I thought you had already left the room when the room service guy came."

"Did you even know that he ordered room service?" I asked while she drove us away from the hotel.

"No. I didn't. I'm thinking he probably did it before I got to his room."

"Yeah, he probably did." I agreed with Shelby while I divided up the proceeds from tonight's mission. Right after I handed Shelby her cut of the money, I stuffed the other portion down into my handbag. She held it up in the air and said, "There's nothing like fucking a dude for some cold hard cash."

I smiled. "And I'm sure you mean that in the most sincerest fashion."

"Why of course." She smiled back. "Too bad, we don't have another dummy lined up for tonight."

"Stop being greedy. One sucker per night is enough. And besides, after that shit that went down tonight, you should be ready to go home and chill." I said.

Shelby laughed at me like I had just made a joke. "You are so fucking paranoid. That guy was just as scared as we were. You heard him when he told us to get out of his room. He wanted us to leave more than we did."

"Yeah, but what if we were dealing with a different guy? Some random asshole that didn't have shit to lose." I pointed out.

"Stop being so dramatic," Shelby said with intentions to downplay the situation.

"How am I being dramatic? You and I rob niggas on a daily basis. And so far we've been on easy street. But, who's to say that our luck isn't going to run out?"

"Tina please don't beat me in the head. We got what we went there for and now we're on our way home. So, chill out will ya'?"

"I 'ma chill out. But so you know, we can't let what happened tonight ever happen again. Agreed?"

Shelby let out a long sigh and then she said, "Yeah. Agreed."

SNEAK PEEK INTO
"I'M NEW YORK'S FINEST PART 1"
(IN STORES NOW)

PROLOGUE

When I first laid eyes on the Federal Agents who were being accompanied by the airport police, I damn near had a heart attack. They were fifty feet away from me. If I wanted to make my escape, then now was the perfect time. Unfortunately for me, every government agent with a badge and gun had every exit in this entire fucking airport blocked off. So the possibilities of me getting away from law enforcement were *slim to improbable*. And even if they weren't, where would I go?

Immediately after I got word that our entire operation blew up in our faces, we got word that the Feds were about to make their arrests, so I was given instructions to go to my place to clean out my safe, erase my hard-drive on my laptop and get my ass over to the hideaway apartment Reggie and I had across town. It was a place no one knew about but the three of us.

Meanwhile, the Feds and the airport police were minutes from closing in on me. I tried to figure out my next step as my heart raced uncontrollably. The edge I had over them was that they were looking for a young woman fitting my description and not a senior citizen woman wearing a grayish colored wig with streaks of black, an old faded blue dress, a pair of orthopedic shoes and walked with a cane. Believe me, I acted the part on queue and used my knowledge of the airport's security system to my advantage. Only a select few of the employees knew the airport was equipped with over a thousand rotating surveillance cameras and fortunately for me, I was one of them. I also knew there were so many cameras that the security staff could not observe them all simultaneously, which immediately prompted me to change my escape plan.

The airport's generator room was only three feet from me. I eased towards the door very carefully. I acted as if I had lost something on the floor and right before I swiped my key card to make my entry, I glanced around the concourse to make sure I was free and clear. When I realized passengers and airline staff had fixed their attention on the manpower search that had engulfed the entire airport, I knew now was the perfect time to make my exit.

Without hesitation, I swiped my key card and pushed the door open. And just when I thought I was about to make a clean getaway, the security alarm went off. Immediately, my body became panic-stricken. I didn't know whether to proceed through the door or turn back around. But as soon as I heard several of the law enforcement officers yell from behind me, I instantly looked back and noticed a horde of law enforcement types rapidly rushing towards me. I could tell by the expressions on their faces that they wanted me badly. I slammed the door shut and looked around the machine-filled room for something I could use to barricade the door. My heart beat at an incredible pace as I scanned and moved around the room. Then I finally saw a pipe lying next to one of the big generators. I snatched it up from the floor and said a quiet and quick prayer as I raced back to the door. I heard the commotion on the other side of the door. There were at least two different voices yelling obscenities as they struggled to get the door open.

"Who has a fucking key card?" I heard one officer yell over top of the loud blaring sound of the security alarm.

That question alone gave me a glimmer of hope that I may be able to prevent them from getting into this room. Now I had to hurry and place the pipe between the crease of the metal bar and the floor. So, when they tried to push the door open, the pipe wouldn't allow the door to move one inch.

Not even ten seconds after I placed the pipe against the door, I heard a loud booming sound hit the door. BOOM! But the door didn't budge. "On the count of three, let's hit it again," I heard one of the officers yell. On the count of three, I watched nervously as they hit the door again. But the door didn't budge. "She's gotta have something barricading the door," I heard another male's voice yell over the top of the continued blaring sounds coming from the alarm system.

Knowing that they had figured out what I had done sent my mind into overdrive. I knew I had very limited time to find my way out of this room before they found a way inside. I had to get a move on it if I wanted to escape this madness.

When I turned around to bolt into the opposite direction, I was stopped in my tracks by a police-issued .40 caliber Glock.

186

"Where the fuck you think you're going?" said a man's voice as he pointed his pistol directly in my face.

The words *slim to improbable* reverberated throughout my mind as I looked down the biggest barrel I had ever been face-to-face with.

INTERNATIONALLY KNOWN

I was elated when the pilot finally landed our aircraft. We had been in the air for five and a half damn hours. The flights from San Diego to LaGuardia were always long and hard on my stomach. Having worked for the airlines for a little over five years, you would think I would be used to it by now. But unfortunately. I wasn't.

What I had gotten used to were the perks of being a flight attendant. A lot of my co-workers weren't aware of it, but I was *New York's Finest*. I was a fly chick from Harlem and I was very popular amongst the men who were elite members of the airline and flew first class. I had them eating out of my fucking hands.

To get straight to the point, I'd befriended and fucked most of them. In return, they'd give me monetary gifts as well as expensive gold and diamond jewelry. Some would say I was being the typical flight attendant, fucking a passenger on every flight. But there was nothing atypical about what I was doing. I didn't consider myself a whore, but this pussy wasn't cheap; hence, the gold and diamond pussy. But the best connections I scored were three passengers who had lucrative drug connections. Unfortunately, after several deals, only one outlasted the other two. His name was Juan Alvarez.

Alvarez was from Costa Rica but he owned a lot of prime real estate here in New York. Not only did he have plenty of money, he had sex appeal. We dated for a few months. During that time I introduced him to my brother, Reggie. Alvarez and Reggie hit it off well and from there, we started a moneymaking enterprise that couldn't be tampered with. While I needed to make more money than the measly $17 an hour I was receiving from the airlines, Reggie needed a consistent supplier and Juan needed someone to put his coke on the streets. So it became a win-win situation for everyone involved.

Alvarez was a womanizer and when I learned that, I cut our relationship short. But we didn't end our business relationship. In the world we both grew up in, money talked and bullshit walked. Juan, Reggie and I had a good business venture, and more importantly, we had a means of transport—my flights to and fro locations across the globe. And as long as I had my bag handlers, TSA agents and mules help get Juan's coke through the airports, he promised he'd continue to supply Reggie and then we all would be happy.

After all the passengers exited our aircraft, my fellow flight attendants, Brooke and Kelsey, inspected the aisles and seats to ensure passengers hadn't left any of their belongings behind. Once that task was completed, we exited the plane ourselves.

I retrieved my Blackberry from my carry-on bag as I entered the airport and called Reggie. I had his number on speed dial, so it only took a matter of seconds to get him on the line.

"What's good?" he asked. He sounded very excited to hear from me. As a matter of fact, he'd always got excited when I called him after I came in from a flight. He knew that once he heard my voice, I had some high-quality product coming his way.

"I hear the cheer in your voice," I told him.

"You damn right! When I hear your voice it makes me happy. Not only do I know that you're home safe, I also know that you've brought home some shit that's going to make us richer than we were yesterday."

I chuckled at Reggie's comment. He was a comedian in his own right. But he was better at selling coke. I introduced Juan to Reggie six months ago and since then, Reggie and I have generated a large sum of cash. I can't count Reggie's money, but I can say that I had saved over two million dollars. I thought about quitting my job as a flight attendant several times, but Reggie stressed over a dozen times how he needed someone on the inside to watch over his investments. He figured that if I left the airline, then he wouldn't have a set of trusting eyes watching to make sure his packages arrived safely into New York. So that's one of the reasons why I was still employed.

"Where are you?" I asked.

"I'm cross town at Malika's apartment. But I'm about to head back uptown because Vanessa's been ringing my Blackberry off the fucking hook. I told her I was out handling business but for some reason, she doesn't believe me."

I chuckled once again. "Come on Reggie, are you listening to yourself? You've cheated on her over a dozen times since you two have been married, so ask yourself why should she believe you?"

He totally ignored my question. The only thing he wanted to talk about was how pure his coke was and how much money he stood to make. And immediately after I gave him the numbers we ended our conversation. Before we hung up, I assured him I would go to the TSA office to check up on the bags to make sure they hadn't been tampered with. And then

I'd put them in the right hands, so he could get them before nightfall.

I had had a long day, but when I looked at how much I had accomplished, I felt good. Normally when I came home from a long flight, I'd take a hot shower and then I'd slip into my terrycloth pajamas and watch a couple of Blue Ray movies. Tonight, I decided to order Chinese and then hit the sack.

While I waited for my Chinese food to be delivered, I got a phone call from my sister-in-law, Vanessa. From time to time she'd pick up the phone to call me when she needed advice on how to handle certain situations with Reggie. I pretty much listened to her take on things, but at the end of the day, my allegiance was with my brother. I would never sell him out even if he were wrong. He was my blood. And whether Vanessa realized it by now, Reggie was going to do what the fuck he wanted and when he wanted, and there's nothing she or I could do to change that.

Reggie has been and always will be a fucking street hustler. Our father was a street cat, so hustling ran through our blood strong. Reggie had stepped the game up big time. He excelled as an athlete in high school—the star running back on our football team and the point guard in basketball. Even then he was a hustler. He ran a betting racket on the football and basketball games he played in. Amazingly, as teenagers, we were raking in bags of dough. As the dude setting the line, and the athlete controlling the results, we always won both on the field and in the streets. And it all computed to one thing—mo' money, mo' money. And that's some real shit!

"Naomi, you need to talk to your brother before I get his ass locked up!" she yelled. Her tone was sharp and I could tell that she was extremely angry. I could also tell that she was pacing the floor in their one million dollar home. She was known for rocking four and a half inch Giuseppe Zanotti heels, so I'd bet money that those were the shoes she rattled the floor with.

"What's wrong? And where is he?" I asked, even though I sensed things were a bit chaotic on the other end of the telephone receiver.

"I'm about to call the motherfucking police on his ass if he puts his hands on me again," she continued to roar.

Before I made one comment, I shook my head in disgust, because there was no doubt in my mind that she ignited this feud with my brother. Vanessa was a fucking drama queen. If the world didn't revolve around her ass, then all hell would break loose. Granted, she was gorgeous and fly. In fact, she looked like a pretty, big booty, small waist chick from Brazil.

But Reggie pulled this chick straight out of one of those projects from Jersey, put her in their luxury, two-bedroom high-rise apartment, laced her with a wardrobe of high-end designers and just recently purchased her a white four-door late model Jaguar with white leather interior. She was the envy of all the chicks from her old neighborhood. However, if they knew everything she had come with a price, they'd switch their focus to something else.

Unfortunately for Reggie, he and Vanessa had been together for close to four years, so he'd have to kill her to get rid of her silly ass. She came into his life when Reggie banked his first million. I'd always believed that timing was everything, so she could not have picked a better time to come into his life.

"Vanessa, put him on the phone," I instructed her because it didn't matter how mad and

upset my brother was, I knew how to calm him down. It took him a few seconds to get on the line but as soon as I heard him ask me what was up, I came back with my own question.

"Reggie, what is going on around there?"

"I'm about to kill this bitch! That's what's going on!" he snapped.

"Reggie, can you calm the fuck down? You got too much shit to handle tonight. So, if you put your hands on Vanessa, she might just call your bluff and dial 911 on your ass this time around. And if she does that, then you won't be able to handle your affairs behind bars."

"The day she calls the police on me is the day she's getting the fuck out of here," he roared in return.

"I know that. And I'm sure she does too, but tonight isn't a good night to be testing the waters. There's a lot of money to be made before sunrise so leave that bullshit alone and get the fuck out of there," I advised him.

"I'm getting ready to leave right now," he told me.

I could tell he was moving through the house, so I was beginning to feel a little at ease. Reggie had just scored a boatload of coke. This package was the come up for the both of us. It was pure as pure can get. And the fact that we got it for a good price made our profit margin skyrocket. See, not only was I a flight attendant, I was also an opportunist. I'd only fuck with you or do something for you if there's something in it for me. A lot of people don't like it, but that's their business. This was my life and I chose to live it the way I wanted.

Marco Chavez, who was Reggie's and my current coke supplier, lived by this same philosophy. In the beginning, I had no idea that he was a coke dealer when I met him on one of our flights from Miami. He had the appearance of a rich real estate investor or a nightclub owner, so money was written all over him. He took my number and the rest was history. That was over a year and a half ago and even though we're no longer fucking, we still had a good working relationship, which was how I intended to keep it.

When money is involved in any situation, you have to put your feelings in your pocket and make the right choice. I learned a long time ago from both my pops and my brother that the only way a woman could survive in this world as if she didn't make decisions based on her emotions. You see men are logical, so they don't get into that bullshit. They come up with a plan and then they execute it. Reggie was known for taking a couple of days to make final decisions. And lately, I've adapted that same method, along with a few others.

When Reggie finally made it out to his car, I let out a sigh of relief because I knew he was about to make his move. "Do you think you're gonna need me to come out to the spot with you?" I asked him after I heard the car door close.

"Nah, I'm straight. Me and Damian will be able to handle everything," he assured me.

"Well, if you need me, just pick up the phone."

"A'ight," he said and then he hung up.

Even after he hung up, I held the phone in my hand, wondering if I should let him do things the way he saw fit. And after mulling over it for a few more minutes, I decided to leave well enough alone.

Normally on my day off I'd lounge around my apartment and catch up on some previously recorded reality shows. But since there was money that needed to be picked up from a few of Reggie's spots, I slipped into a pair of blue denim shorts and accented it with my *I'm Proud to be a Puerto Rican* t-shirt, although I'm half black as well. I topped it off with a cute pair of old-school Adidas sneakers. Every now and again, I'd go back to my roots and get into my 'hood wear.

On a more serious note, I had to fit the part when I rolled out to Reggie's spots to handle my business. Mostly everyone in the 'hood knew me, but that's not who I was worried about. From time to time, the narcotics detectives would bribe their way into the apartment of one of the elderly tenants in the buildings of the project and set up surveillance operations. So if I ever went there looking as if I didn't belong, then I'd immediately become their next target. And I can't have that. I had invested too much into our operation to have one slip up such as that fuck up everything. And it was equally important because one day very soon I had planned to take all the money I had saved and leave the country for good.

On my way out of my luxury apartment, I grabbed my keys, my Yves Saint Laurent sunshades, and handbag, and marched on to the elevator. Down in the lobby area of my building, the doorman saw me approaching the exit door and rushed to open it.

"How are you doing this morning Ms. Foxx?" he asked.

"I'm doing great Sam. Thanks for asking," I replied as I made my way out of the building. Like clockwork, my vehicle was parked out front and ready for me to get on the road.

I'm a huge fan of Lil Wayne, so I hit the power button for my eight-disc CD player and turned up the volume on *How to Love.* The hook on this track had my head rocking from one side to the next. And when it ended I hit the repeat button and listened to it three more times until I got to my destination, which was Harlem, my old stomping grounds. The block surrounding the Polo Grounds was crowded with cats trying to get their paper. I recognized a few of the locals and smiled at them after I exited my car.

"Can you keep an eye out for my baby?" I asked no one in particular, referring to my new midnight black Mercedes GL550 SUV.

"You know we gotcha' ma," I heard one of the guys say. I couldn't call any names, but I knew their faces all too well. And they knew me, which was what counted most. They also knew that I wasn't to be fucked with. Being a Foxx gave me recognition and status, which meant I could leave the car running and no one would touch it. My brother Reggie laid down the law from day one and every one of these cats who patrolled the Polo Grounds knew the consequences if his law was broken. I was certainly off limits. No one could harm one little hair on my sweet ass body. Not to mention they also had to ensure no one else from the outside of this compound fucked with me, my whip or anything I was transporting. Or they had hell to pay.

The compound consisted of four buildings that we called the Four Towers. The Towers had been there ever since I could remember. As a child, my mother and hustler father used to warn us about hanging out at the Towers. It was where the action was, and that action at some point over time had moved from one tower to the next.

After one of the guys assured me I had nothing to worry about, I proceeded to make my rounds. The first stop was to this chick's apartment that was in the first tower. Her name was Candie and she lived on the sixth floor. When I entered the lobby, I was met by two of Reggie's marksmen, or shall I say the lookout patrol.

Each building had its own lookout patrol. Ben and Dre' were both big guys standing around six feet tall and not easy on the eyes. But who cared how they looked, they weren't paid to stand around and look pretty. Their job was to make sure no one came into the building that shouldn't be there while I made my rounds. Reggie made sure his men were fully armed with heavy artillery when I entered into each of the four towers. And after I made my presence known, they greeted me and moved out of the way.

"Be back in a minute," I told them and then I headed for the elevator. I was lucky the elevator was working. Most times the elevator would be out, and I hated those days when they came. I was in excellent shape and did my share of walking getting from point A to point B in the numerous airports I had traveled through. But walking up six, seven or ten flights of stairs was not my idea of fun or staying in shape.

As I approached the elevator door, it opened and out came a very familiar face. This familiar face was Angel. Angel was a chick Reggie once used to hold his dope packages until she messed around and allowed her twenty-year-old baby brother to steal several grams out of each package so they could sell it to make an extra profit. When Reggie found out about it, he made sure her brother never walked again and she only walked with one arm. Thank God he listened to me and didn't have them killed. He did make an example out of them though. After I smiled and said hello, I continued onto the elevator.

When I reached the sixth floor, I was met by two more of Reggie's patrolmen. Lucky, the patrolman I was very familiar withheld the elevator door open as I stepped out into the hallway. Then he prevented the elevator door from closing to prevent anyone else from getting on the elevator. This was a precautionary measure Reggie instructed them to take to protect me and isolate me from riding in the elevator with anyone else while I made my rounds to pick up his dough. You never know if he had enemies out to interrupt his business or worse, hurt someone close to him— namely me. So far it had worked as advertised.

"Lucky, you look like you're working hard?" I commented.

"Most definitely. I do this all day, every day," he smiled. Reggie gave him the name Lucky because his short ass had been shot twice and both times he escaped death. Now he had a metal plate in the back of his head. Although he pretended the plate didn't bother him, I knew it did. I had caught him go into a zone. His eyes would glaze over and you could tell he was in another world. And during this time, he would go the fuck off, most times for no reason at all. I witnessed him beat the hell out of his baby mama for no reason.

It's rumored that he received a disability check every month for his condition. So regardless of his short height, a lot of cats out here didn't fuck with Lucky. We all knew he really was certified crazy.

The other brother was Walter, Walt for short. Reggie had just put him on the payroll, so he was new to our team. He was kind of cute, and he was definitely my type. But he was the help. And I didn't fuck the help. Equally, and probably more importantly, Reggie didn't play that. Too bad for Walt, because we probably would've made some serious chemistry in my king-size slay bed.

Like clockwork, as soon as I knocked, Candie opened the door to let me in, then she closed the door behind me. We proceeded directly to the kitchen of her small apartment and she handed me a manila envelope filled with cash. Different day, same procedure every time.

"It's all there," she assured me.

"I'm sure it is. But you know I always count the money in front of you just so we can be on the same page. But when you tell me that everything is here and then I go behind you and find out that you are short, then that's not a good look."

"I understand," she replied in her childlike voice.

Candie wasn't your typical ghetto chick. She was a very pretty Puerto Rican, a mother of one, who spoke very good English, and she was very ambitious. With a five-year-old son, she managed to find a way to hustle for Reggie during the wee hours of the night and pursue her Bachelor's degree in marketing doing the day. I was shocked when I entered her place over a year ago and noticed she was doing homework. It completely blew me away. And from that day on, I had mad respect for this chick. She was a twenty-four-year-old mother handling her business, who also had plans to pursue her Master's degree. From previous conversations, I knew she was saving money so she could move out of this place and give her and her son a better quality of life. She was all right in my book.

After I finished counting the money, I winked at her and said, "You're right. It's all here."

She smiled back and said, "I told you so." She escorted me back to her front door and I stuffed the envelope inside my handbag before I made my exit. I never left out of anyone's apartment with the money in my hands. That's a big no-no. After I reentered the hallway, Lucky was front and center while Walt stood by the elevator with his hands holding both sides of the sliding doors.

"You a'ight?" Lucky asked.

"Yeah, I'm cool," I replied.

"You ready for me to escort you back downstairs?"

"I'm ready as ever."

"Well, let's do it then," Lucky smiled as he walked alongside me towards the elevator. Walt held both doors of the elevator open until Lucky and I were safely inside. Once inside, Lucky assured him that he'd be right back as the doors closed.

Lucky pressed the button for the first floor and I actually admired the seriousness in his face. He took his job to heart. I was his mission for now and I felt safe in the elevator with Lucky.

When the top door of the elevator was snatched open and two masked men jump down inside of the elevator, one after the other, tumbling down on top of Lucky, I damn near pissed myself. We were both caught off guard. I screamed as loud as I could and got hit in the mouth with the butt of one of the guy's pistols. I fell hard against the elevator wall.

"Stop the elevator," one guy instructed the other, as he took Lucky's Glock from him. I looked down at poor Lucky. He was knocked the fuck out. I was all alone in this fucking elevator with these two motherfuckers and had no idea what was about to happen next.

They managed to stop the elevator on the third floor. And before I could blink an eye, the guy who snatched Lucky's gun from him, pointed the exact same gun in my face and demanded that I give him the money I had just picked up from Candie's crib. So without hesitation, I handed him the manila envelope and begged him to let me live.

"Oh, you don't have to worry about that. I'm gonna let you live this time. But the next time you might not be so lucky," he said. Then he did the unbelievable, he aimed Lucky's gun at him and shot him directly in his face. His entire head blew up like a fucking melon. Blood splattered all over me and the walls of the elevator. And as I began to scream once again, that's when both men fled off the elevator.

I swear I had never been that afraid in my life. Fear had gripped my whole body. I was afraid to move one inch. I wanted to get up and press the button to close the elevator door but my entire body was paralyzed. And all I could do was cry as I watched Lucky's head ooze blood onto the floor around him. I couldn't believe I had just witnessed Lucky get killed just like that. He and I were just talking a few minutes before all this shit went down and now he's dead.

Oh my God! What am I going to tell Reggie? And the police for that matter. I knew they're going to question me like I was an accomplice. I just hoped that whatever they decided to do, they didn't put my name in the fucking local new papers or mention it to the media that I was in the center of this murder investigation. This wouldn't look good for my employers at the airline. They wouldn't understand why I was out here at the Polo Grounds. Everyone in the state of New York knew the reputation of the Polo Grounds.

That thought, thinking about the airline and my possible firing and overall humiliation brought me back to life. The best way for me to avoid all of the unnecessary drama and publicity was to get a grip and woman up. I wiped my fucking tears and got the hell off the floor. My mind was on cops and homicide detectives arriving before I could get the fuck out of there. I tried my best not to touch anything. I literally lifted myself from the floor without using my hands and then I used my elbow to press the first-floor button.

Then came the waiting—I swear it felt as if the elevator was taking forever to get to the first floor. When it finally stopped and the doors opened, I burst out of the elevator like I was in serious need of some oxygen. Both Ben and Dre rushed towards me.

"What the fuck happened? You been shot?" Dre wondered aloud.

I tried to hold back my tears but the floodgates to my ducts burst out. "No, I didn't get shot. This is Lucky's blood. He was shot in the head by two guys with masks," I sobbed.

Ben rushed over to look inside the elevator. "Oh shit! She ain't lying. That nigga Lucky's brains are hanging out of his fucking head!" Ben replied, hysterically.

Dre left my side and rushed to the elevator to see Lucky's dead body for himself.

I stood there helplessly. I didn't know whether I was coming or going. All I wanted to do was get out of there.

"Who did this shit to him?" Dre rushed back and asked me. I could tell that he was ready to make the guy who did this pay.

"I don't know. They both wore black ski masks," I continued to sob.

"Where did they come from?" Ben wanted to know.

"They were on the roof of the elevator. And as soon as we got on the fifth floor, they busted from the door, robbed me for the money I got from Candie, killed Lucky and then they stopped the elevator on the third floor and ran off," I explained.

"Where is Walt?" Ben asked.

"He's still on the sixth floor, I think."

Ben looked at Dre. "Cover her up and take her to her truck and then call Reggie, while I run upstairs to the sixth floor to see where that nigga Walt, is," he instructed Dre.

"I'm on it." Ben insisted and then we watched as Dre' ran off.

The End!